By Phil Bildner

The Rip and Red Series

A Whole New Ballgame
Rookie of the Year
Tournament of Champions
Most Valuable Players

The Sluggers Series
with Loren Long

Magic in the Outfield
Horsin' Around
Great Balls of Fire
Water, Water Everywhere
Blastin' the Blues
Home of the Brave

pictures by TiM PRoBeRt

MENT
MPIONS

SQUARE
FISH

Farrar Straus Giroux
New York

SQUARE
FISH

An imprint of Macmillan Publishing Group, LLC
175 Fifth Avenue
New York, NY 10010
mackids.com

Our books may be purchased in bulk for promotional, educational, or
business use. Please contact your local bookseller or the Macmillan Corporate
and Premium Sales Department at (800) 221-7945 ext. 5442 or by
e-mail at MacmillanSpecialMarkets@macmillan.com.

Library of Congress Cataloging-in-Publication Data

Names: Bildner, Phil, author. | Probert, Tim, illustrator.
Title: Tournament of champions / Phil Bildner ; pictures by Tim Probert.
Description: New York : Farrar Straus Giroux, 2017. |
    Series: Rip and Red | Summary: Rip, Red, and their friends on the
    Clifton United basketball team travel to a spring sleep-away tournament. |
    Description based on print version record and CIP data provided by
    publisher; resource not viewed.
Identifiers: LCCN 2016035880 (print) | LCCN 2017012645 (ebook) |
    ISBN 9781250158437 (paperback)   ISBN 9780374305086 (ebook)
Subjects: | CYAC: Best friends—Fiction. | Friendship—Fiction. | Basketball—
    Fiction. | Contests—Fiction. | Family life—Fiction.
Classification: LCC PZ7.B4923 (ebook) | LCC PZ7.B4923 Tou 2017 (print) |
    DDC [Fic]—dc23
LC record available at https://lccn.loc.gov/2016035880

Originally published in the United States by Farrar Straus Giroux
First Square Fish edition, 2018
Book designed by Andrew Arnold
Square Fish logo designed by Filomena Tuosto

3 5 7 9 10 8 6 4

AR: 3.7 / LEXILE: 530L

For Wes and Andrew,
captains of team Rip & Red
—P.B.

For Mom and Dad
—T.P.

One-on-One-on-One

"Next basket wins," I said, clapping for the ball.

"No," Diego said. "Win by two."

"Win by two, Mason Irving," Red said as he spun around the pole under the basket.

Diego, Red, and I were the only three in the Reese Jones Elementary schoolyard. All the other kids were waiting at the car pickup line or getting on the buses to go home.

"Yo, it's always win by two at RJE," Diego said.

"How do you know?" I said. "You never play."

I'd never seen Diego play hoops before, which is why I had no idea he could ball. Seriously ball.

"Ten for Diego Vasquez, ten for Mason Irving." Red pointed at me. "It's always win by two at RJE."

"Whose friend are you?" I said.

"Both!" Red let go of the pole and hopped from foot to foot.

Red's my best friend. He calls everyone by their first and

last name. To him, I'm Mason Irving. To everyone else, I'm Rip. It's a basketball nickname.

I placed the ball on my hip and shook out my dreadlocks.

Diego shook out his hair, too.

"Here's the scene," Diego said, smiling. "You're lying on your bed, and rhino dung is dripping from the ceiling. It's all over you. It's on your face. It's even in your mouth."

All game long, Diego had been talking trash, mocking me, and saying nasty stuff.

I cut right, got a half-step on him, and took a shot from inside the elbow. It clanked off the back of the rim.

"You tried, son." Diego grabbed the rebound and dribbled to the top of the key. He gestured with his chin at Red. "Time for me to finish off your little friend."

"I'm taller than you are," I said.

I lunged for the ball, but Diego blocked my hand with his shoulder. He then spun past me and drove in for a layup.

"Boom! In your face!" he shouted.

"Eleven for Diego Vasquez, ten for Mason Irving," Red announced.

Diego toe-flipped the ball off the cement and jogged to the top of the key. "You're going down, son," he said.

"We'll see."

"It's next basket now." He shook out his hair again. "Check." He passed me the ball.

I punched it back.

Diego swung the ball back and forth by his shins. He wanted to go left—Diego was a lefty—so I gave him the right.

He drove left, but instead of going lower-the-shoulder hard like he had been all game, he backed me down. A couple steps from the hoop, he put up a shot.

It bounced off the front rim. I boxed him out for the rebound.

"Who's your daddy?" I said, dribbling out.

"Go, Mason Irving!" Red shouted.

"Time for me to stick a fork in your butt," I said. "You're done, *son*."

Diego wasn't the only one chirping. I'd been dishing out the trash talk as much as he had.

"It's Irving's turn," I play-by-played. I love doing play-by-play. "Vasquez had a chance to put this one away, but he left the door open. Irving slides right and sizes up the court. He dribbles baseline . . . He shoots . . ."

"No good!" Diego bodied me for the board. "Now it's Vasquez's turn," he said, mocking my announcing. "Watch him stick a fork in Irving's butt and show him who's really done."

Diego lowered his shoulder and drove left. He put up a shot and banked it in.

"Ballgame!" He pounded his chest and stomped across the paint. "Who's your daddy now?"

Red laughed along. "Who's your daddy now?"

Diego stepped to Red. "What are you laughing at?" he said. "Now it's time for me to dispose of *you*."

"Me?" Red pointed to himself.

"Yeah, you." Diego gripped the pole under the basket and spun around. "Time for me to beat you at free throws."

"Ha!" I said. "This I'd like to see."

Red's a free-throw-shooting beast. I've seen him hit twenty and thirty in a row tons of times. When Red's locked in at the line, he's money.

"First one to miss loses," Diego said, backpedaling to the line.

"Make him shoot underhanded," I said to Red.

"Oh, yeah." Red shook his fists by his shoulders. "You have to shoot underhanded, Diego Vasquez."

That's how Red shoots his free throws. He goes through this whole routine and then shoots the ball underhanded.

"Underhand, overhand, behind the back, whatever." Diego bobbed his head.

I tossed him the ball. "No pressure."

Diego glanced at Red and then placed his toes on the line. He power-dribbled a few times and spun the ball in his hands like Red does before he takes his foul shots.

"No pressure," I said again.

Diego shot the underhanded free throw. It banged off the backboard without hitting the rim.

"Ha!" I laughed. I pounded my chest and stomped across the lane like Diego had a minute ago. "Ballgame!"

"Yo, Red still has to make his," Diego said.

"Put him away," I said to Red, and then spun back to Diego. "Watch how it's done, *son*."

Red set himself on the line and trapped the ball under his left foot soccer-style. He took several breaths, picked up the ball, and squared his shoulders.

"I could say some wack things right now," Diego said, leaning in. "You want to hear some wack things?"

It didn't matter what Diego said. Red wasn't hearing any of it. He was locked in.

Red dribbled three times low and hard and stood back up. Then he spun the ball until his fingers were right and looked at the rim. He extended his arms and took the shot.

Underhanded.

Swish!

"Boo-yah!" I hammer-fisted the air.

"Bam!" Red cheered. He smiled his super-wide basketball smile. "Who's your daddy now, Diego Vasquez?"

Road Trip

"The free-throw-shooting machine strikes again!" someone said.

We all turned.

Our teacher, Mr. Acevedo, was jogging onto the court.

"Well done." He gave Red a pound.

"Thanks, Mr. Acevedo."

Mr. Acevedo's the coolest and best teacher we've ever had. All the fifth graders think so.

Mr. Acevedo had asked Diego, Red, and me to wait for him until after Thunder Dome. That's what he calls the car pickup line during dismissal. Mr. Acevedo has Thunder Dome duty every afternoon.

We walked over to the Amp, the amphitheater at the far end of the playground. The Amp's where Mr. Acevedo sometimes holds Teacher's Theater Time. That's when he reads to the class. Mr. Acevedo tries to read to the class every day. Right now, he's reading us *The Fourteenth Goldfish*.

"Let's get right down to business," he said. He sat on the front bench and faced the three of us. "So I spoke to all your—"

"Wait for me!"

We all turned again.

A girl was running toward us.

"It's Maya Wade!" Red waved his arms like a football referee at the end of a play. "Maya Wade's here."

Maya played with us on our basketball team, Clifton United, but because she didn't go to RJE, I hadn't seen her since the season ended back in the fall. I couldn't believe how tall she was. We used to be the same size, but now she had five or six inches on me, like almost all the other fifth-grade girls.

"Hey, boys." She straddled the seat next to Mr. Acevedo. "Did I miss anything?"

"Not at all," he said. "Perfect timing."

"Long time no see," Diego said to her.

She smiled. "Very."

I checked Diego. I didn't know he and Maya knew each other.

"How was school?" Mr. Acevedo asked Maya.

"The same," she answered. "I brought Carolina to Maker-space." Carolina was Maya's little sister. "Someone will drop her at the house afterward."

"I'll let Aisha know."

Aisha was Mr. Acevedo's girlfriend. Sometimes she met Mr. Acevedo at school. I didn't know they knew Maya outside of basketball.

"I asked Maya to join us," Mr. Acevedo said. He strummed his legs. "Let's get back down to business. So I spoke to all your moms."

"That's never a good sign," I said.

"For the record," Diego said, holding up his hands, "I had nothing to do with sticking the juice box straws up the first graders' noses. Not this time."

"I'll make a note of it," Mr. Acevedo said. "Relax, Diego. No one here's in any trouble."

To be perfectly honest, when Mr. Acevedo said he spoke to all our moms, I did get a little tingly, because I didn't exactly have a squeaky-clean record this year. Back in the fall, I got into this thing with Avery Goodman, this girl in my class who uses a wheelchair and sometimes gets an attitude (but now we're friends). Then a bunch of us—including Diego, Red, and Avery—got in trouble for Operation Food Fight (which was actually pretty cool and creative). Then I got into this other thing with Tiki Eid, the new girl on the basketball team (but she's no longer here).

"Clifton United is taking a road trip," Mr. Acevedo said. Mr. Acevedo is also coach of our Clifton United basketball team. "We've been invited to play in a tournament of champions."

"Ballin'!" Maya banged her hands like cymbals.

"Outstanding!" I said.

"Oh, yeah!" Red said. "Outstanding."

"So why am I here?" Diego rested his arm on my shoulder. "I'm not on Clifton United."

"Well, Diego, that's what I spoke to your mom *and* uncle about," Mr. Acevedo said. "They both said you could join the team."

"Don't play, Mr. Acevedo," Diego said.

"I'm not playing."

"I'm not well, you know."

"Actually, you are well, Diego." Mr. Acevedo tucked his hair behind his ears. "That's why you can play, if you want to."

"I want to, I want to, I want to!" Diego pounded the bench with both fists. "Yes, yes, yes!" He jumped up and danced in circles on the bench. "It's about time they let me off my leash!"

For a while, Diego was sick, really sick. He missed the whole second half of third grade and the beginning of fourth. When he came back to school, he always wore hats, goofy ones with earflaps and tie strings, because his medicines made his hair fall out.

"I got to shoot around with Diego over the weekend," Mr. Acevedo said to me. "So did Maya. We ran into his family at the park. I had no idea he could ball."

"Neither did Rip," Diego said, pretending to tomahawk-dunk on me. He sat back down. "I schooled him!"

I ruffled Diego's hair. Red ruffled his hair, too.

Diego had hair now. Even though he stopped wearing his hats a few months ago, I'm still not used to seeing him without them. Every time I look his way, I expect to see a black-and-white dog with huge brown eyes peering into my soul or a one-eyed blue-and-yellow Minion staring a hole into my brain.

"Yes, yes, yes!" Diego pounded the bench again. "I can't

believe my uncle's down with this. He never lets me do anything."

"Both your mom and your uncle are on board," Mr. Acevedo said.

"But how am I allowed to play?" Diego asked. "I wasn't on the team in the fall."

"We got you a health waiver," Mr. Acevedo said.

"Sweet," Diego said.

My basketball brain started to churn. I couldn't wait to play in the same backcourt as Diego. I loved playing with lefties, especially lefties who knew what to do. Diego was also nonstop movement. Just like me. If Diego had been on Clifton United during fall ball, we wouldn't have just made the playoffs, we would've won the whole thing.

"Let me tell you about the tournament," Mr. Acevedo said. He crossed his legs and grabbed his ankles. "It's called the Jack Twyman Spring Showdown, and it takes place at the Hoops Haven Sports Complex. Sixteen teams have been invited. It's two rounds of pool play followed by a single-elimination knockout stage. Every team plays a minimum of three games."

"This is going to be sick," Diego said, bobbing his head.

"Who else is on the team?" Maya asked.

"From fall ball, it's the four of you, plus Mehdi Karmoune. The rest of the roster is kids from teams we played against."

"Are they trying out?" I said.

"Not enough time." Mr. Acevedo shook his head. "The Showdown's Easter weekend. Less than two weeks from now." He tapped my knee. "We're counting on you big-time, Rip. We need you to pick up where you left off at the end of fall ball. You're Clifton United's floor leader, our team general. I'm going to be pushing you hard, real hard."

"Bring it," I said.

Mr. Acevedo faced Red. "Suzanne and I had a long conversation about the tournament," he said. Suzanne is Red's mom. "I know she spoke to you about it."

Red shook his fists by his ears and nodded.

"You know about the tournament?" I nudged Red. "How come you didn't say anything?"

Red shrugged.

"I gave Red and Suzanne a heads-up," Mr. Acevedo said. "I've learned not to spring things on Red out of nowhere, right?"

Red turtled his neck.

"Suzanne's okay with you going," Mr. Acevedo said. "Ms. Yvonne is going to be one of the chaperones. She'll be there the whole time."

Ms. Yvonne is the special ed teacher who's worked with Red ever since pre-K. All the fifth graders know Ms. Yvonne. Whenever she pushes in during class, she helps all the kids.

"It's about a two-hour bus ride," Mr. Acevedo said. He adjusted a hoop at the top of his ear. "We'll be taking a real bus and staying overnight in a hotel."

"This is going to be sick!" Diego said.

Red bounced his knees and pressed his elbows to his sides.

"You don't have to make up your mind about it now." Mr. Acevedo tapped Red's leg. "And even if you decide not to come, you're still Clifton United."

"For real," I said.

"No matter what you decide, you'll still practice with the team," Mr. Acevedo said. "Just know that we want you to come. Clifton United wants you there."

Red plays for Clifton United, but he doesn't *play* for Clifton United. Not in games. Though the two times he did see action this year, he was clutch city!

Red's quirky. Not just with basketball—with everything. He needs things to be a certain way, and when they're not he has a bad time. But compared to how he was at the beginning of school, Red's gotten so much better. And compared to how he was last year and the year before, he's like a different kid.

"We still need to find a third chaperone," Mr. Acevedo said. "Hopefully, that won't be a problem."

"What about Mehdi's dad?" I said.

Mehdi's father came to almost every Clifton United game. Even away games.

"Unfortunately, he has a prior work commitment," Mr. Acevedo said. "This evening, I'll send out the email with all the rules, forms, practice schedules, and everything. You'll have to wait until practice tomorrow to find out about your new teammates." He drew a circle with his finger around the four of us. "You in?"

I hammer-fisted the air. "Boo-yah!"

No More Earplugs

Whenever Red and I walk to and from RJE, we always talk about school or YouTube or Xbox or the NBA. But heading to my house this afternoon, Red barely said a word. He kept his head down and patted the sides of his legs with his fists.

He'd been that way ever since Mr. Acevedo mentioned the hotel. Up until fourth grade, Red never stayed anywhere without Suzanne. But last summer, he began sleeping at my house. Now he does a lot.

This trip would be his first time somewhere else without Suzanne.

Across the street, a man was walking his dog. The dog had an orange Frisbee in its mouth.

"The puppy's got a purse," I said.

Red didn't look up.

"When I get my dog," I said, "I'm teaching it all kinds of cool tricks."

Nothing.

"I'm going to teach it to poop in the toilet."

Red glanced my way.

"Ha!" I pointed. "Just checking to make sure you're listening."

"I'm listening, Mason Irving," he said softly.

"My mom's friend taught her dog to pee in the shower," I said. "She lives in an apartment building and doesn't have a backyard. So sometimes, instead of taking the dog for a walk, she lets it pee in the shower and then rinses it down the drain." I bumped his shoulder. "Maybe if I teach my dog to pee in the shower, my mom will let me pee in the shower."

"I doubt it."

I laughed. "If I teach my dog to poop in the toilet, I'll let you wipe its butt."

"No thanks, Mason Irving."

Red grabbed the stop-sign pole at the corner and spun around. On the way to my house, we pass two stop signs and eight streetlights. Red spins around each one.

We crossed the street.

"We're taking a real bus to the tournament," I said. "A Clifton United team bus. How cool is that?"

Red began patting his legs again: pinky-thumb, pinky-thumb, pinky-thumb.

"I bet the courts at Hoops Haven are regulation courts," I said.

He hunched his shoulders.

"We're going to meet so many cool kids. I bet a lot of them are NBA freaks like you."

Red loves the NBA. If you ever want to know about a player or a team or a famous game, just ask Red.

"I bet we get some serious swag." I soccer-kicked a patch of dandelions and watched the fluff float off. "Serious swag."

Still nothing.

I let out a puff. Red had to come to the tournament. No way was I letting him miss it. He would have such an amazing time. Probably better than everyone combined.

I bumped his shoulder. "Maybe Steph Curry will be staying at our hotel."

"Why would Steph Curry be staying at our hotel?"

"Maybe all the Warriors will be."

The Golden State Warriors are Red's favorite team. He liked them way before they started getting good. His favorite player—even more than Steph Curry—is this old-school guy named Rick Barry, who shot his free throws underhanded and wore number twenty-four.

Red wears number twenty-four.

"Why would all the Golden State Warriors be at our hotel, Mason Irving?"

"Maybe they heard about Clifton United's free-throw-shooting machine and they had to come see the legend in person." I held out my fist. "No more earplugs."

He gave me a soft pound. "No more earplugs."

Red doesn't like loud noises, and whenever he played basketball, he always wore earplugs. They were even part of his free-throw routine—when he took his deep breaths, he placed his fingers over them. But recently he stopped wearing them.

"You're an assassin from the foul line," I said. "Now we

need to turn you into an assassin from three-point land. As deadly as Steph Curry."

"Steph Curry is deadly from three-point land," Red said, half smiling.

"I hope Diego can dial it up from long distance." I pretended to crossover-dribble. "He knows how to handle the ball, that's for sure."

"Even better than you."

"Dag." I shoulder-bumped him again. "I'm still taller than him."

"Not by much, Mason Irving."

"So? I don't get to say I'm taller than a lot of kids."

Red laughed. "Especially the girls."

"Especially the girls!" I shook out my hair. "Did you see how tall Maya got?"

"Maya Wade got very tall."

"Every fifth-grade girl towers over me. They're all humongous!"

"Humongous!"

"Humongous and ginormous!"

Mom Being Mom

"What have you done to my son?" Mom said. She stopped halfway down the basement stairs and grabbed the handrail like she was about to faint.

"Very funny, Mom," I said.

"What happened to Mason Irving?" Red asked without looking away from the TV. He was playing Xbox.

"That can't possibly be my son," she said.

I was folding my laundry. I used to never go *near* my laundry. But lately when I see my dirty clothes on my bedroom floor or on the kitchen counter or on the stairs or on the couch—I leave my clothes everywhere—I'll sometimes put them in the hamper or wash. I'll also take my clothes out of the dryer and fold them.

I don't know what's gotten into me.

"If you want me to stop, I will," I said.

"No, no, no," Mom said, walking the rest of the way down the steps. "You can do my laundry next, if you like."

"Mom! That's disgusting!"

Red laughed. "Mason Irving would love to do your laundry, Rip's Mom."

Rip's Mom. That's what Red calls my mom.

"Keep talking." I balled up a sock and chucked it at Red. It sailed over his head. "I'll seriously mess with your score."

He rocked his gaming chair. "You couldn't if you tried."

"You want to see me mess with—"

"Bam!" Red sank a bank shot off the sidewall of the arena. "Mason Irving would love to do your laundry, Rip's Mom." Red laughed again. "Tell her what we were doing with—"

"Don't go there, Red," I said.

"Don't go where?" Mom asked. "What have you two been up to?"

I grabbed my glow-in-the-dark smiley-face boxers and dangled them in front of Red's face.

He swatted them away.

I definitely didn't want Mom to know what we'd been up to. Before she came down, we'd found two of her bras mixed in with the sheets and towels. I'd put one on and stuffed it with socks, but I couldn't get it to stay up. Red had made a slingshot. Then we'd jumped around on the couch with the bras on our heads.

"So tell me about this tournament." Mom sat down on the Rubik's Cube table beside Red.

"The Jack Twyman Spring Showdown," he said, still staring at the game. "Do you know who Jack Twyman was?"

"Blake Daniels does," I said.

That's Red's real name, Blake Daniels.

But the kid who lives and breathes the NBA hadn't known who Jack Twyman was until he got on YouTube a few minutes ago.

"Jack Twyman played for the Rochester Royals and the Cincinnati Royals in the 1950s and the 1960s," Red said. "Jack Twyman was an NBA All-Star six times. Jack Twyman was inducted into the Naismith Memorial Basketball Hall of Fame in 1983."

"Sounds like he was quite the ballplayer," Mom said.

"Do you know what Jack Twyman is most famous for, Rip's Mom?" Red didn't wait for an answer. "Jack Twyman is most famous for helping Maurice Stokes. Maurice Stokes was his teammate on the Rochester Royals and the Cincinnati Royals. Maurice Stokes suffered a head injury in a basketball game and was paralyzed. Jack Twyman helped take care of Maurice Stokes for the rest of his life."

"I guess that's why the Spring Showdown is named after him," Mom said.

"That's why the NBA has the Twyman-Stokes Teammate of the Year Award," Red said. "The Twyman-Stokes Teammate of the Year Award recognizes the league's ideal teammate, who exemplifies selfless play and commitment and dedication to his team."

Mom and I laughed. Red was repeating word-for-word what he'd just read. Red does that a lot. He does it with the lunch menu at school all the time.

"Chauncey Billups won the Twyman-Stokes Teammate of the Year Award in 2013, the first year the NBA had the award," Red said. "Shane Battier won the Twyman-Stokes Teammate of the Year Award in 2014, the second year the NBA had the award. Tim Duncan won the—"

"Is it okay for Diego to play basketball?" I asked Mom, to cut Red off. If I hadn't, he would've shared every last detail about the award.

"It's not like he's contagious," Mom said.

"Cootie Man!" I dove onto the couch.

Last year, when Diego came back to school after being sick, there was a big class meeting for kids and parents. At the meeting, Diego kept touching everyone and calling himself Cootie Man. It's how he showed everyone we weren't going to catch what he had.

Mom had helped arrange the meeting. She's the principal at River West, a middle school a few towns over. All the fifth-grade parents know she's a principal, so whenever things come up at RJE, they always look to her.

"If Diego's mom and uncle are fine with him playing," Mom said, "I'm sure it's okay. I've had similar situations with kids at my school."

"Diego knows how to play ball," I said. "I had no idea he was so good."

"I remember when you two played on the same soccer team back in first grade," she said. "Or maybe that was kindergarten. He was perpetual motion. The both of you were."

"That's what Diego's like playing basketball," I said. "He never stops."

"Diego Vasquez plays basketball like Rip Hamilton," Red said.

"*I* play basketball like Rip Hamilton." I pointed to myself. "That's my nickname."

My nickname comes from Rip Hamilton, the old-school Detroit Pistons player who never stopped moving on the court. My number is thirty-two, the same as his.

"You should see the way Diego Vasquez dribbles," Red said.

"Hopefully, I will," Mom said.

"He also likes to talk," I said.

"Talk?" Mom asked.

"Trash talk," I said. "He's always chirping. You should hear some of the things he says."

"Have you two read Coach Acevedo's email?"

"No, Rip's Mom," Red said.

Mom looked at me.

"I've been doing laundry." I grinned wide. "If you want me to sit in front of a screen instead of helping out with—"

"Wow!" She cut me off and pointed a twirling finger at my face. "That charming smile of yours right now reminded me so much of your father. It was uncanny."

I flinched. Mom hadn't mentioned my father in at least

a couple weeks. He didn't live with us. It was just Mom and me. I liked it better that way. Much better.

"I know you don't like me bringing him up," she said, "but I had to point that out. Anyway, Coach Acevedo sent the tournament packet, or should I say the tournament *book*. I can't believe the number of forms they make you fill out and . . . What am I talking about? Of course I believe it. The amount of paperwork we deal with at my school is absurd. We're so busy amassing data, we can't even sit down with students and—"

"Mom," I interrupted, "you're having a conversation with yourself."

"I can always count on you to set me off on a rant."

"Just doing my job."

"The two of you need to fill out the forms Coach Acevedo sent. I suggest you don't wait until the last minute." She leaned forward so Red could see her face. "Did you hear what I said?"

" 'The two of you need to fill out the forms Coach Acevedo sent,' " Red repeated. " 'I suggest you don't wait until the last minute. Did you hear what I said?' "

I laughed. "I guess he heard you."

"Have you decided if you're going?" Mom asked Red.

He hunched his shoulders and swayed from side to side.

"Staying in a hotel with your teammates sounds like a lot of fun," she added.

"No, Mom," I said, shaking my head. "Not now."

"You'll be in a room with Rip and two other boys," she went on. "I'm sure Suzanne will talk to their parents. Before the trip, maybe the four of you—"

"Mom, not now."

Red squinched his face.

"Ms. Yvonne's going. I know she—"

"Mom, stop!"

Finally, she listened.

"Oh, honey, I'm sorry," she said, rubbing Red's back. "We don't have to talk about this now. We can do it another time."

I twisted a lock near my forehead at its root. I didn't want Mom talking to Red about the tournament. I didn't want *any-one* talking to him about it. I had to be the one to convince him to go. People don't know Red like I do. They think they do, but they don't.

"Honey, I'm sorry," she said again. "We can do this another time."

Red pressed his elbows to his sides and nodded.

Mom stood up and stepped in front of the television. "I must say, I am a little surprised at you two," she said, her tone brightening. She pinched her thumb and index finger together. "I thought you'd be a teeny-tiny bit more curious about who's on the team."

"We're curious," I said.

She picked up the sock I'd thrown at Red and behind-the-back-tossed it into the laundry basket. "Then why haven't you checked Coach Acevedo's email?"

"He's not telling us who's on the team until practice tomorrow," I said.

"Is that so?" Mom headed for the stairs. "Well, if you *do* decide to read his email, you may discover someone thought it might be better if families knew who was on the team ahead of time."

Red and I dove for my laptop.

Roster, Unexpected

"Eduardo Lopez?" I said, reading the screen. "That's Super-Size from Millwood."

"Why would Coach Acevedo put Eduardo 'Super-Size' Lopez on Clifton United?" Red asked.

"He's friends with Mega-Man. That's the kid who knocked out Keith during fall ball." I pointed to the next name. "Bomani Taylor? That's Elbows from Millwood. That kid plays so dirty."

"Why would Coach Acevedo put Bomani 'Elbows' Taylor on Clifton United?"

I wondered the same thing as Red. Yeah, Super-Size and Elbows could ball, but they both played for Millwood. No one liked those kids. Why *would* Coach Acevedo put them on Clifton United?

"There's only twelve kids on the roster," I said, counting the names. "One, two, three, four of them are girls. Holly Winston's on the team. That's Speedy from Rolling Hills."

"Holly 'Speedy' Winston ran you off the court, Mason Irving."

"Thanks for reminding me." I shoulder-bumped him. "Zoe Reynolds and Mimi Santos from Yeager are the other two girls."

I didn't know much about them. When we played Yeager in the fall, Red and I weren't there because of what happened with Operation Food Fight. I was thinking they had to be decent since we lost. Plus, they were fifth-grade girls. They had to be humongous and ginormous.

I checked the last two names—Hudson Moss from Edgemont and Julian Crawford from Harrison. Hudson was a big body, and Headband (that's what they called Julian because he always wore one) could shoot and play D.

In my head, I replayed Coach Acevedo's words: *We're counting on you big-time, Rip. We need you to pick up where you left off at the end of fall ball. You're Clifton United's floor leader, our team general. I'm going to be pushing you hard, real hard.*

"This is going to be sick!" I said, pounding the carpet.

"We're the Clifton United All-Stars," Red said.

"Yes! The Clifton United All-Stars!"

Part of the Plan

Tweet! Tweet!

"Let's circle up," Coach Acevedo said.

The twelve members of the Clifton United All-Stars gathered around Coach Acevedo at midcourt of the RJE gym for the start of the first practice the next day after school.

"Show of hands," he said. "How many of you have played in a tournament like this before?"

No hands went up.

"That's what I thought," he said. "We leave for the Showdown a week from Friday. That means, between now and then, we have our work cut out for us. That means we need to get busy."

Red clapped hard. "We're getting busy. Bomani 'Elbows' Taylor and Julian 'Headband' Crawford are getting busy. Eduardo 'Super-Size' Lopez and Holly 'Speedy' Winston are getting busy—"

"Whoa, whoa, whoa, hold up there, Red," Coach Acevedo said. "Let's discuss these nicknames from fall ball. I want to make sure everyone's comfortable with them. Headband? Elbows?" He looked at Julian and Bomani. "You okay with them?"

They nodded.

"Everyone else okay with the nicknames?" Coach Acevedo looked at Super-Size and Speedy. "If not, you need to let me know. You can do so now, or you can do so privately. Okay?" He soccer-style-kicked up a basketball and underhanded it to me. "Rip, we're expanding Clifton United's pregame tradition. It now includes practices. Will you explain our tradition to everyone?"

I dribbled to the middle. "Before the start of every game," I said, "our free-throw-shooting machine over here takes a foul shot." I nodded to Red. "Now he's going to take one before the start of every practice."

Diego rested his arm on Red's shoulder. A few months ago, if someone had even tried touching Red like that, he would've freaked. But not anymore.

"Red doesn't play in games," I said, dribbling back and forth between my legs. I'd been practicing that all winter and finally had it down. "But Red's Clifton United like everyone else. Everyone brings value to Clifton United."

"Thanks, Mason Irving," Red said, smiling his mega basketball smile.

"He's in on every drill," I added, "but don't bang and body him."

Coach Acevedo clapped for the ball and punched my pass right to Red. "Go take your shot."

"Thanks, Coach Acevedo," Red said.

"Yo, light it up!" Diego bounced like he had springs in his sneakers.

Red stepped to the line and trapped the ball under his foot. He took several breaths and picked up the ball. Then he squared his shoulders and looked at the front rim. He dribbled three times—low and hard—and stood back up.

With my basketball eyes, I checked Coach Acevedo. On the way back from recess today, I'd asked him if we could expand Clifton United's pregame tradition to practices. He loved the idea. It was part of my Get-Red-to-Come-to-the-Showdown Plan.

Coach Acevedo pumped his fist.

At the line, Red spun the ball until his fingers found the right seams and looked at the rim again. He extended his arms and took the free throw.

Underhanded.

Swish!

"Bam!" Red cheered.

Tweet! Tweet!

"We're all business now." Coach Acevedo drew a circle in the air with his finger. "Let's get our game faces on. Let's get poppin'."

Running the Offense

I stood beyond the three-point line at the top of the key and sized up my five: Zoe was playing the two (shooting guard), Diego was at the three (small forward), Headband was at the four (power forward), and Maya was at the five (center). Yeah, Maya was our center. That's how tall she now was.

We were going over Black Widow, a play in our half-court offense. I was at the one (point guard). I was running the show. I was the floor general.

"Our minds are working hard," Coach Acevedo said. "Everyone's learning every role, everyone's learning every position." He pointed to Maya. "Right now, you're at the five, but when we go small, you may be running the point. Or you might be at the two or three." He clapped twice and pumped his fists. "Every role, every position."

For less than a nanosecond, I thought-bubbled the play:

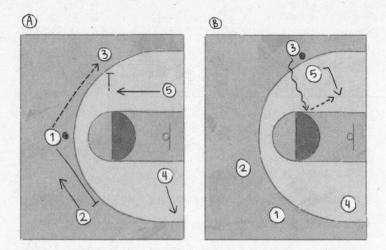

My basketball brain computed:

- *I (1) pass to Diego (3) and cut to Zoe (2).*
- *Maya (5) slides up, pops out, and sets a back screen for Diego to block his man as Diego goes to the hoop.*
- *Diego dribbles right.*
- *Maya seals off Diego's man and rolls to the hoop.*
- *Headband (4) clears out to free up the lane.*
- *Diego drives for the layup or dumps the ball to Maya for the layup.*

"Here we go," Coach Acevedo said.

Tweet! Tweet!

"Black Widow!" I called.

I whipped the ball to Diego and cut right.

"It's Vasquez time," Diego said to Mehdi, who was guarding him. "Later, son."

He jab-stepped left, waited for Maya to set the screen—a screen Mehdi had no chance of getting around—and then blew by him. As he drove down the lane, Hudson slid over to help, but not before Diego got off the shot and sank the layup.

"Boss!" Diego beat his chest and stomped to me. We did a jumping hip-bump. "We run this floor."

"Ballin'!" Maya clapped her hands like cymbals.

Tweet! Tweet!

"Let's settle down," Coach Acevedo said. "You executed a play in practice, but you're acting like you won the Larry O'Brien Trophy, and if you don't know what the Larry O'Brien Trophy is, look it up when you get home."

I knew what the Larry O'Brien Trophy was. Red's told me a gazillion times. It's the Super Bowl trophy of the NBA.

"Way to go, Diego Vasquez!" Red cheered.

"Boss!" Diego pumped his fists.

Diego was also part of my Get-Red-to-Come-to-the-Showdown Plan. His job was to include Red as much as possible. That way, Red would realize he'd be missing out if he didn't go. Red doesn't like missing out on anything.

"You didn't draw Hudson far enough from the hoop," Coach Acevedo said to Headband. "He almost cut off Diego's lane. Complete your assignments on defense." He clapped twice. "Let's run that again. Match up. Here we go."

Tweet! Tweet!

I fired my pass to Diego. Once again, he caught the ball and waited for Maya's screen. This time, Mehdi fought through it. Well, not really. Diego still got a step on him. In the lane, when Hudson slid over, Diego passed to Maya, who'd rolled around Mimi to the hoop. She sank the layup.

"Ballin'!" Maya shouted.

"Boom! In your face!" Diego thumped his chest again. "We're two for two!"

Tweet! Tweet!

Coach Acevedo pointed at Headband. "You still didn't draw your man out far enough."

"Person," Maya said. "There are guys *and* girls on Clifton United."

Coach Acevedo nodded and turned to Mimi, who was guarding Maya. "You can't lose track of your *person* that close to the hoop." He looked at Diego and me. "Way to run the offense."

Above and Beyond

"You looked great out there today, Rip," Coach Acevedo said as he rolled the basketball rack past where I was sitting on the floor.

"Thanks," I said.

He waved for me to join him. I finished putting on my sweats and hoodie, popped up, and followed him to the storage closet by the stage.

"That was some steal you had against Diego," he said. "I may have to try that move one time."

I knew exactly the play he was referring to.

I was on defense guarding Diego. We were going over Quicksilver, another half-court offense play. Diego was chirping and talking trash again, but I wasn't about to let what happened in the schoolyard yesterday happen at practice today. No way. When he tried driving on me, I reached in low, smacked the ball up, and snatched it out of the air.

"The two of you looked terrific out there together." Coach Acevedo pulled open the closet door and rolled the rack next to the orange cones.

"Thanks," I said again.

"Now I need you to go next-level." Coach Acevedo stepped from the closet. "Let's have a conversation."

We sat on the front of the stage under the basket.

"I need you to go above and beyond," he said.

"Above and beyond?"

"We only have a few practices to prepare," he said, brushing some of the long hair off his face. "We can't afford any missed assignments. There can be no lapses in focus. Everyone needs to be on point."

"Got it."

"Expect a few changes come Thursday," he said. "I'm already making decisions. I'm looking to you and counting on you out there, Rip."

"No worries, Coach," I said.

"I liked what I saw from Elbows and Super-Size."

"They were both much cooler than I thought they'd be."

"It's got to be hard for them," he said. "They had nothing to do with what went down with their Millwood team last fall. Unfortunately, when anyone looks at them—anyone who knows about it—it's the first thing that comes to mind."

With my thumb and index finger, I twisted a lock above my ear. I knew exactly what Coach Acevedo was talking about. Whenever I looked at Super-Size and Elbows, a screaming image of Coach Crazy popped into my head. That's what I called Millwood's coach because of the way he always carried on when we played. Red was terrified of the guy. Then over the winter, I heard that Coach Crazy completely lost it and started a fight with a ref. A fistfight. The police had to be called. It made the news.

But here's the thing: at practice today, when I looked at

Super-Size and Elbows, Coach Crazy *didn't* pop into my head. Not once.

I was in full basketball mode.

"Make sure everyone's on board with them," Coach Acevedo said. "We don't have time for anyone not to be." He stared at the empty basketball court. "Red looked fantastic out there."

"Red looked awesome."

"He seemed to really enjoy playing with Maya."

Red and Maya were paired up together at practice. During passing work, Coach Acevedo had them demonstrate the different passes before each drill. Then during rebounding work, they were boxing-out battle buddies.

"How's it going with him?" Coach Acevedo asked. "Do you think he'll—"

"He's coming." I answered the question before he finished it. "He has to come."

"Whatever I can do to help, you let me know."

"Thanks."

"I meant what I said in the Amp yesterday." He leaned back on his hands. "I'm going to be pushing you hard, Rip."

I swung my legs. "I'm up for it, Coach."

"You ever hear of the author Virginia Euwer Wolff?" he asked.

"I don't think so."

"When you get to middle school next year, find her books. Her book *True Believer* has one of my all-time favorite lines: 'We will rise to the occasion, which is life.'"

"I like that," I said.

"I want that to be Clifton United's mantra."

"Mantra?"

"Our team motto." He sat back up and drummed the front of the stage. "I want that to be our rallying cry. We will rise to the occasion, which is life."

"We will rise to the occasion, which is life."

Perky's Post-Practice

"What kind of dog would you get, Mason Irving?" Red asked.

"A boxer," I said. "Or a pit bull."

"Oh, yeah. I love pit bulls."

"Definitely a rescue dog."

Red placed a finger on the paper napkin and spun it around on the table. "Definitely a rescue dog."

We'd stopped at Perky's on the way home from practice. That's the coffee shop we go to all the time. Red and I sat at our usual table in the front. Mom and Dana sat at their usual table in the back. Dana's an assistant principal at another school in my mom's district. Mom's been seeing her since the fall.

"What about you?" I asked. "What kind of rescue dog would you get?"

"I'll know it when I see it," Red said.

"I like that."

I'd just finished inhaling a cheesecake brownie. I popped a handful of leftover crumbs into my mouth and checked the barista behind the counter. He had ginormous Batman plugs that made it look like he had holes in his earlobes. They freaked out Red, which was one of the reasons why he had his back to him. The other reason was that he always sat facing the door.

"Practice was sick today," I said.

"Oh, yeah, Mason Irving. Practice was sick."

"You sank that free throw and set the tone." I drummed the table. "Money!"

"You had that steal against Diego." Red spun the napkin faster. "The play of the day!"

"Who's your daddy now?"

We both laughed.

"I can't wait to play in the same backcourt with Diego," I said.

"Diego Vasquez and Mason Irving are going to be un-stoppable."

"U-N-S-T-O-P-P-A-B-L-E." I held out my fist.

He gave it a pound.

"You have to be there, Red," I said.

He hunched his shoulders.

"I'm serious," I said. "You can't miss this. You know you want to go."

He squinched his face and swayed from side to side.

"Everyone wants you there. Diego wants you there. Maya wants you there. I want you there. It's going to be sick."

I stopped. I knew better than to press the issue any further.

"You should read this when I'm done," I said. I held up *The Greatest: Muhammad Ali*, the book I was reading for choice.

"I like Walter Dean Myers books," Red said. He relaxed

his shoulders. "You should read *Fast Sam, Cool Clyde, and Stuff.*"

"So do you want a boy dog or a girl dog?"

"A girl dog," Red said. "Definitely a girl dog."

"Why's that?"

"Because boy dogs pee on you!"

I laughed. "No, they don't!"

"Yes, they do, Mason Irving. Boy puppies lift their legs and pee on everything! Boy puppies lift their legs and pee on fire hydrants. Boy puppies lift their legs and pee on bushes. Boy puppies lift their legs and pee on furniture. Boy puppies lift their legs and pee on people!"

At the exact same moment, Red and I stood up, lifted our legs, and pretended to pee like boy dogs.

Teach Can Ball

At recess the next day, we played four-on-four: me, Diego, Melissa, and this fourth grader, Connor, against Jordan, Declan, Miles, and this other fourth grader, Trevor.

Our four got off to a slow start, but once Diego and I found our rhythm we were *unstoppable*. We ran a couple sick give-and-gos, and on one play I hit Diego with a backdoor pass that faked out Trevor so bad he scraped his palms on the pavement.

Right now we were up 10–6. Point game. We were on defense. I was doing the play-by-play.

"Declan with the ball up top," I said. "He dishes to Jordan on the right. Jordan sends it back to Declan. Wow, that offense looks lost out there. Declan passes to Miles in the corner. Miles takes a quick shot . . . No good!"

Melissa boxed out Jordan for the rebound and whipped the ball to me. As I dribbled out to the top of the key, my basketball eyes spotted Diego cutting baseline. I fired a one-handed pass his way. He caught it under the hoop, shoulder-bumped Trevor, and sank the layup.

"Boo-yah!" I hammer-fisted the air.

"Ballgame!" Diego shouted. "Boom! In your face!"

We did a jumping hip-bump.

"Picking on the little kids, Diego?" someone said.

We all turned.

Mr. Acevedo was jogging onto the court.

"I am a little kid," Diego said.

Mr. Acevedo clapped for the ball. Diego pump-faked twice before passing it.

"Let's see you try a move like that on me." Mr. Acevedo spun the ball on his finger.

"A little game of one-on-one?" Diego said, rolling his neck.

"Careful, man." Declan slid next to Diego. "Teach can ball."

Mr. Acevedo could seriously ball. Back in the winter, he played for the teachers in the fund-raiser basketball game against the varsity hoops team. He was the game's high scorer.

"I can ball, too." Diego rested his arm on Declan's shoulder and nodded to Mr. Acevedo. "Let's see what you got, Teach."

Mr. Acevedo let the ball spin off his finger and trapped it under his foot. He then slipped off his bracelets, took the larger hoops out of his ears, and handed his jewelry to Miles.

The whole class stood along the baseline. I was between Red and Avery under the basket.

"What are we betting?" Diego bobbed his head.

"We're not betting," Mr. Acevedo said.

"Chicken?" Diego flapped his elbows.

Some of the kids laughed.

"No betting," Mr. Acevedo said.

"No basketball either," Avery said, wheeling forward. "All I hear is chitchat." She bumped the back of Diego's leg. "Play the friggin' game."

Diego bounced up and down like he had springs in his sneakers. I thought about what it must've been like for him not being able to play ball for so long and what it must've been like not knowing if he'd ever run ball again. No wonder he was so amped every time he took the court.

"What are we playing to?" Mr. Acevedo asked.

"First basket wins," Diego said, still grinning.

"No."

Diego flapped his elbows again. "Chicken?"

Everyone laughed.

"Not chicken." Mr. Acevedo kicked up the ball. "Smart. Even *you* are capable of sinking some ridiculously lucky shot. But you're not capable of getting lucky like that twice." He patted his chest. "Not against me. First to two wins."

"Whose ball?" Diego asked.

Mr. Acevedo backpedaled to the top of the key and took a shot.

Swish!

"Oh!" A bunch of kids shouted.

Mr. Acevedo patted his chest again. "My ball."

"Way to shoot, Mr. A.," a kid named Zachary said.

"Teach can ball!" Red hopped from foot to foot.

I cupped my hands around my mouth. "You got this, Diego!"

"Dude, take Mr. Acevedo down!" Avery called.

A few kids started clapping.

"A grown man taking on a boy with cancer," Diego said. "Yo, that's messed up."

"You don't have cancer anymore, Diego," Mr. Acevedo said.

"Acute myeloid leukemia. Taking on a boy with AML. That's so messed up."

"Talk all you want," Mr. Acevedo said, smiling. "It's not going to make a bit of difference."

Diego rolled his neck. "You know I'm in your head."

He was in *my* head. It freaked me out when Diego joked about his cancer.

"Enough with the friggin' chitchat!" Avery shouted. "Play the game!"

"Check." Mr. Acevedo underhanded the ball to Diego.

Diego underhanded it back harder. "Ball."

Mr. Acevedo lowered his shoulder and blew by Diego. He smacked his hand against the backboard as he sank the layup.

"Nice defense," Mr. Acevedo said.

"Who's your daddy, Diego?" I laughed.

"That's only one." Diego held up a finger and then pointed it at me. "Only one, *son*." He picked up the ball and flipped it to Mr. Acevedo.

"Check." Mr. Acevedo punched it back.

Diego squeezed the ball. "You want to hear something wack? One time, my uncle's dog ate his rope toy, and the next day when the dog went to poop, he couldn't go. My uncle had to pull the rope strings out of the dog's—"

"Didn't you hear Avery?" Mr. Acevedo cut him off and motioned to the ball. "Enough with the friggin' chitchat. Let's play."

Diego underhanded it back even harder than last time. "Ball."

Mr. Acevedo drove again, but this time Diego was ready. He reached in and got his fingers on the first dribble. Mr. Acevedo lost the handle. Diego scooped up the ball and, in one motion, spun toward the basket and threw up a prayer.

Swish!

"Boom! In your face!" Diego ran along the baseline and smacked hands with everyone. He smacked mine the hardest. "Who's your daddy now?"

Daddy.

The word donged the inside of my head like a clocktower bell.

My father.

Out of nowhere, Mom had mentioned him the other day. Now I was thinking about him again.

I bopped the side of my head and shook myself back to the schoolyard.

"Next basket wins!" Avery rolled forward. She leaned back in her chair, popped a wheelie, and did a three-sixty.

As cool as it was seeing Diego play basketball, it was even cooler seeing Avery *into* basketball. Up until fifth grade, she'd never even been to a game. But ever since she went to her first Clifton United game back in the fall, she's been hooked. This coming summer, she is going to try wheelchair basketball.

"Close it out, Diego!" Xander McDonald called.

"Finish him off," Attie Silverman said.

Next basket won. Diego had the ball.

"One time when I was in the hospital," he said, bobbing his head, "this girl projectile-puked all over everyone. The social worker's face and hair were covered in puke. Covered, Mr. Acevedo!" He bounce-passed the ball to him. "Check."

"You really think I'm going to let you beat me in front of everyone?" Mr. Acevedo said.

He soft-tossed the ball back to Diego, and as soon as he caught it, Mr. Acevedo swarmed. He batted the ball *up* and out of Diego's hands.

Just like I did to Diego yesterday.

"I'll take that!" Mr. Acevedo said, plucking the ball from the air. He stared down Diego. "You got anything else to say?"

Mr. Acevedo didn't wait for an answer. He backed Diego into the paint and shoulder-bumped him aside. Then he pivoted left and put up the shot.

Swish!

"Who's your teacher?" Mr. Acevedo stood over Diego. He bobbed his head and beat his chest. "Boss!"

Rising to the Occasion

"This here is Amy Wu," Coach Acevedo said at the start of Thursday's practice after school at RJE. Clifton United had circled up under the basket by the water fountains. "She'll be taking Headband's spot on the roster."

"Headband's not on the team anymore?" I said.

"No, he's not," Coach Acevedo said.

I clasped my hands and pressed my thumbs and knuckles to my lips. Coach Acevedo had said to expect changes, but I had no idea that meant kids might be replaced.

"That's five girls now." Maya folded her arms and nodded. "Ballin'."

"Everyone needs to be on point today." Coach Acevedo looked around the huddle and made eye contact with a few kids. "We come committed to excellence."

"Committed to excellence." Diego jumped in place and shook out his arms.

I sized up Amy. She played in a different league, but I'd

seen her run ball a couple times. She had real good hands and a pretty good shot, and, like Maya, she'd gotten a lot taller.

"Decisions are being made." Coach Acevedo looked around the huddle again. This time, he made eye contact with me. "Dazzle me. I like to be dazzled." He soccer-style rainbow-flicked the basketball to Red. "Shoot your free throw."

Red took his free throw.

Red made his free throw.

Tweet! Tweet!

"Rip, put everyone in pairs," Coach Acevedo said, pointing downcourt. "Make two lines under the basket facing this way."

"A-Wu's with me," I said. That's what other kids were already calling Amy. I started walking to the hoop. "Elbows, you're with Mehdi."

"I'm with Red," Maya called.

"Oh, yeah." Red hopped. "I'm with Maya Wade."

"I'm with Super-Size." Diego leaped onto his back.

I lined up first under the hoop. "Hudson, you're with Zoe. Mimi, you're with Speedy." I clapped three times. "We will rise to the occasion, which is life."

"Yo, where'd you learn that?" Diego stepped to me and laughed in my face. Literally laughed in my face. "That was mad corny."

Everyone else laughed, too.

I cringed.

"Where'd you learn it?" Diego asked again.

"A fortune cookie?" Elbows said.

Everyone laughed more.

"Coach Acevedo," I said.

"Seriously?" Diego stopped laughing.

I nodded. "He wants it to be our team saying, our mantra."

"That's tight," Diego said. "Mad corny, but tight."

I checked Coach Acevedo. He was adjusting the mini cones at the far end of the court and hearing all of this.

I cringed again.

"We will rise to the occasion!" Diego began jumping in circles. "We will rise to the occasion! We will rise to the occasion!" He chest-bumped Elbows and then ran along the baseline until he reached Red. "We will rise to the occasion!" He double-high-fived him. "We will rise to the occasion, which is life!"

"We will rise to the occasion, which is life!" Red said, and hopped.

Everyone laughed harder.

I checked Coach Acevedo again. He was laughing, too.

Clifton United Can Ball

"**Clifton United can ball!**" I said to Diego and Speedy during the water break between end-of-practice sprints and end-of-practice free throws.

"This is what I call a team!" Speedy said. "You're fearless under the boards." She double-fist-bumped Diego. "Fearless."

"That was tight," he said, bouncing like always.

"You outjumped Super-Size!" Speedy said. "On that one play, you got the rebound over him and then scored on that crazy pass from Elbows. Fearless!"

But it was more than just that one play. Diego and Speedy put on a show all practice. The two smallest kids on the team played bigger than everyone.

"You're a menace on defense," Diego said to Mimi as she walked up. He gave her a pound.

"A menace!" Speedy hopped to Mimi and double-fist-bumped her as well.

Diego pivoted to me. "You've got the insane-in-the-membrane crossover dribble."

"The Iverson crossover!" I air-dribbled. "Unstoppable."

"Yo, check out Red," Diego said, resting his arm on my shoulder.

Red was talking with Maya by the stage, hopping from foot to foot and basketball-smiling.

I pumped a fist by my side. Maya was now part of my Get-Red-to-Come-to-the-Showdown Plan, too. Her job was to make Red feel like an indispensable member of Clifton United, something Maya was doing even before I told her about the plan.

"He has to come to the Showdown," Speedy said.

"He'd better come to the Showdown," Mimi added.

"Trust me," I said. "Red's getting on that bus next Friday." I shook out my hair and turned to Elbows and Super-Size, who had joined us. "Coach Acevedo's a little different from your coach, right?"

"A little?" Elbows said.

"He's usually not this intense," I said. "This is the most—"

"You call this intense?" Elbows cut me off. "Coach Acevedo's a playful puppy compared to our old coach."

"Coach Acevedo's a playful puppy dog," Diego baby-talked.

We laughed.

"I can't understand how you played for Coach Crazy," Speedy said.

"He was the only parent available," Super-Size said.

"Whose parent was he?" I asked.

"Our big guy," Elbows said. "The one who almost cracked open that kid's head."

"Coach Crazy is Mega-Man's dad?" I held up my hands. "No way!"

"Yeah," Super-Size said. "Coach Roth is Charlie Roth's dad."

"No way!" I said again.

"Is Mega-Man anything like his father?" Speedy asked.

Super-Size shook his head. "He's real quiet. No one liked hanging with him because of his dad."

"I thought you were good friends with him," I said.

"Not me," Super-Size said.

"Me neither," Elbows added. "I never knew what to say to him, especially when his dad was losing his mind."

"Which was all the time," Super-Size said. "But what bites is now we have no coach and no team."

"Yo, you have a team." Diego rested his arm on Super-Size's shoulder. "You have Clifton United."

In the Zone

Twenty-two hours and sixteen minutes later...

"Let's talk about the zone defense," Coach Acevedo said at Friday's practice, once Clifton United huddled up and after Red sank his beginning-of-practice foul shot. "How do we beat it?"

Red's hand shot up. Coach Acevedo chin-nodded to him.

"To beat a zone defense, players on offense should stretch the defense," Red said. "Players on offense should perform shot fakes and pass fakes. Shot fakes and pass fakes lead to opportunities."

Coach Acevedo twirled his whistle. "Looks like someone did his homework."

"Oh, yeah, Coach Acevedo," Red said.

That big tournament packet Coach Acevedo had sent out on Monday included a section on attacking the zone.

"Players on offense should keep proper spacing," Red went on. "Proper spacing spreads the defense and forces the defense to cover a lot of ground. Proper spacing leads to op-portunities."

"He makes his free throws *and* comes prepared." Coach Acevedo snatched his whistle. "Let's give this a whirl. Ladies, the five of you are on offense."

Maya clapped her hands like cymbals. "Let's show them how it's done."

"Speedy, you're running the point," Coach Acevedo said. "Go set your team." He spun to me. "Rip, you're leading the defense. Set up in a two-three zone."

"Who's in?" I asked.

"Your call."

"Elbows, Mehdi." I waved them over. "Red, Diego. Let's do this."

We huddled near midcourt.

"Could you have picked a smaller five?" Diego asked.

"I like small ball." I bumped Diego's shoulder. "You play down low in the middle since you're our biggest player."

"Diego Vasquez isn't our biggest player," Red said.

I reached to ruffle his hair, but Red ducked away.

"You're too slow, Mason Irving," he said, smiling and pointing.

Up until this year, I would never have tried ruffling Red's hair. He would've freaked. But now he's fine with it. He ruffles my hair, too.

"Time to show Coach Acevedo we're committed to excellence," I said. "Time to do a little dazzling."

"Let's show them this small-ball five gives Clifton United the best chance at winning." Diego gave everyone double pounds. "We will rise to the occasion, which is life."

We all laughed.

As we set up in our zone, my basketball brain revved:

- *Watch the shot fakes. Watch the pass fakes.*
- *Don't bite when they try to spread the floor. Don't chase the ball. Play your space.*
- *Watch Mimi and Zoe going high post to low post. No open shots in the paint.*
- *Don't let Speedy penetrate. Don't let her create openings.*
- *Box out.*

Tweet! Tweet!

Our zone was airtight!

The girls couldn't get us to chase the ball. They couldn't get the ball into the paint. They didn't score a single basket. They didn't get a single offensive rebound.

Lockdown!

"Nicely done, defense," Coach Acevedo said after five straight stops. "That's what we want to see."

Tweet! Tweet!

"Let's switch it right up!" Coach Acevedo said. "Defense, you're on offense. Let's go."

Our small-ball five huddled at the top of the key.

"We move the ball around quickly," I said. "No one stands still." I pointed to Red and Elbows. "One of you is getting the open shot in a short corner."

Diego smacked the floor with both palms. "Let's do this, offense," he said. "Let's show the girls how it's really done."

We whipped the ball around the perimeter and looked for gaps, but the girls' zone was in perfect sync.

So it was time for a little dazzling.

Elbows passed to me on the wing. I looked inside for an open teammate or for a gap in the zone. Nothing. But instead of sending the ball to Hudson up top or back to Elbows in the corner, I fired an overhead skip pass across the court to Diego. He sent the ball to Red, wide open in the corner. Red squared to shoot, but *his* basketball eyes spotted Elbows sliding into the paint. Red fed him with a sweet pass. Elbows put up the shot.

Swish!

"Great look!" Diego pounded the floor with his fist. "That's how it's done."

"It sure is," Coach Acevedo said, clapping. "Way to make the extra pass, Red. Beautiful play, offense. Beautiful!"

"Boo-yah!" I hammer-fisted the air.

"Bam!" Red cheered.

* * *

"Let's learn a couple of those out-of-bounds plays you sent me," Coach Acevedo said later at practice. "Zoe, Rip, Red, Speedy, Maya—thanks for the suggestions. They were exactly what I was looking for."

Coach had messaged us last night:

Clifton United:

At ⊕⊕ 2morrow, we'll b working on out-of-bounds plays. I'm looking for suggestions. If u know any good ones, text, call, or email me at acevedo@cliftonunited.com. Try 2 get it 2 me this eve or first thing in the morn. ⊕⊕

Coach Acevedo

I'd emailed Coach Acevedo my play suggestion as soon as I got his note. I didn't know Red had suggested one until right now.

"Speedy, we're learning yours first." Coach Acevedo tossed her the basketball.

"Sweet!" she said.

"We're calling it Hawkeye." He pointed the rest of us to the baseline. "Take it away. Teach your teammates."

She ran the ball out to the foul line and power-dribbled once with both hands. "Hawkeye is an under-the-hoop out-of-bounds play," she said. "When it works, you don't just get the ball in, you score a basket."

Speedy taught us the play. She ran to each spot on the floor and demonstrated the positioning and moves. Then she ran through the entire play by herself, showing us all the passes, shots, and options.

"Everyone got all that?" Coach Acevedo asked. "Good," he said, before anyone could answer. "We'll be running it shortly." He called for the ball and trapped Speedy's pass under his heel. "Our other out-of-bounds play is a sideline play. We're calling this one Thor. Maya, you're going to teach it to us."

"This play is boss!" She banged her hands like cymbals. "It works every time."

"But before you start," Coach Acevedo said, "I have to

acknowledge the most creative suggestion I received." He fired a chest pass to Red. "If we ever need a desperation play at the end of a game, we're running yours."

"Thanks, Coach Acevedo." Red squeezed the ball.

"You want to tell everyone a little about it?"

"Oh, yeah." Red hopped from foot to foot. "The play is called Pacer. That's what Valparaiso—"

"Valpa who?" Diego interrupted.

"Valparaiso University," Red said. "On March 13, 1998, the Valparaiso University Crusaders won their first ever NCAA tournament game, defeating the University of Mississippi Rebels seventy to sixty-nine on a buzzer-beater three-point shot by Bryce Drew."

"That's the play you suggested?" Maya asked.

"That's the play, Maya Wade."

"Now that's boss!"

"The Valparaiso University Crusaders were the number-thirteen seed in the 1998 NCAA tournament," Red said, still hopping from foot to foot. "The University of Mississippi Rebels were the number-four seed in the 1998 NCAA tournament. The University of Mississippi Rebels were expected to advance to the second round, but—"

"I'm going to cut you off there, Red," Coach Acevedo said. "You are going to teach us Pacer, just not right now. Definitely before we leave for the Showdown. And I'm putting you on notice. If and when the time comes we need a close-out play, you're the man."

"Thanks, Coach Acevedo." Red hopped faster. "I'm your man."

Dazzling

I chugged what was left in my water bottle and wiped the water from the sides of my mouth with my shoulder sleeve. In a couple minutes, we were running our end-of-practice up-and-backs. On my select team last year, we called them by a different name, but Coach Acevedo wasn't a big fan of that word. No matter what you called them, they were brutal.

"Way to go, Rip," Coach Acevedo said, walking up. "Above and beyond."

"Thanks," I said, smiling.

"I'm serious, Rip. You far exceeded my expectations. Impressive."

My smile grew. "You said you like to be dazzled."

"And you sure did dazzle. Things are gelling." He play-punched my shoulder. "Once we finalize our third-chaperone situation, we'll be good to go."

"We still don't have someone?"

"Not yet." He shook his head. "We have a few options. It'll all work out."

"Do you know anything about the other teams?" I asked.

"I know some of them have been playing together for years."

I chucked my water bottle toward the corner. It landed against the rolled-up volleyball nets. "Have you seen them play?"

"Not in person." Coach Acevedo tucked his hair behind his ears. "How we fare may depend on the luck of the draw. Some of these teams are supposed to be . . . impressive."

"Like me."

"Like you." Coach Acevedo smiled. "Like Red. That was some pass he made to Elbows."

"Amazing!"

Coach Acevedo laughed. "I got such a kick out of the play he suggested."

"He didn't tell me he sent you one."

"You think he's coming to the Showdown?"

"He's coming. I know Red."

"I know you do. You're a good friend."

"He's a good friend."

"The way you interact with him," he said, poking my chest, "is impressive. Red makes such a difference. Everywhere he goes. You're a big part of that."

"Thanks," I said. "I think . . . Coach Acevedo, I think you'd make a good dad."

"Wow, Rip. Where'd that come from?"

"I don't know . . . I just . . . I think you would. You listen to kids, and you . . . and you compliment people." I shrugged. "I don't know. I just think you would."

"That's a kind thing to say, Rip." He held out his fist. "Thanks."

I gave him a pound.

"Aisha and I hope to start a family in the not-too-distant future," he said. "She works with a number of foster agencies. That's how we got involved with Maya and her sister and their situation."

I didn't know there was a situation. It helped explain why Maya was with him in the park the day he ran into Diego.

"For the moment," Coach Acevedo went on, "we're letting life happen as it happens." He play-punched my shoulder again. "By the way, saying nice things to me isn't getting you out of up-and-backs."

"It was worth a shot," I said.

A basketball rolled into the back of my leg. I turned. Diego chased it down.

"Thanks, Coach Acevedo," Diego said.

"Thanks for what?"

"For everything. For basketball, for Clifton United, for everything. Thanks."

Coach Acevedo looked at me. "Did you put him up to that? Did you tell him to say something—"

"No!" I held up my hands and smiled. "I swear I didn't!"

"Tell me to say what?" Diego said.

"Rip's been over here saying kind things to me, and then you show up and do the same."

Diego bobbed his head. "Your backcourt duo is in perfect sync," he said.

"Your *unstoppable* backcourt duo is in perfect sync," I added.

"Well, just like I told Rip," Coach Acevedo said, "sweet-talking me isn't getting you out of your up-and-backs."

"Yo, I want to run." Diego rested his arm on Coach Acevedo's shoulder. "Bring on the up-and-backs. I've wanted this for the longest time."

Ping Ping

Ping. Ping.

Mom reached for her cell.

"Don't do it," I said, pointing a sweet-potato fry.

She pulled back her hand.

Mom, Red, and I were at the kitchen counter eating dinner in our usual spots—I was closest to the cabinets, Red was next to me, Mom was facing us.

Ping. Ping.

"Don't do it, Rip's Mom." Red swiveled his stool. "The use of cell phones is strictly prohibited during meal time."

Mom raised both hands.

That was the rule. Suzanne and Mom came up with it (along with like a gazillion other rules) when Red and I finally got cell phones last Christmas. During dinner, everyone's phone goes in the metal pail at the end of the counter.

Suzanne and Mom have a much harder time with the rule than Red and I.

"What's your avatar?" Mom asked Red.

"Don't try to trick him," I said to her.

"I'm not trying to trick anyone."

"She's trying to get you to look at your phone," I said. "Don't fall for it."

Red swiveled faster. "My avatar is a Labrador retriever puppy."

"Just like Rip's."

"Mason Irving has a boxer avatar."

"A boxer puppy." I took a bite of my turkey burger.

"Do you change your avatar as often as Rip does?" she asked.

"Red changes his avatar more than he changes his underwear!" I answered first.

Ping. Ping.

Mom leaned in and read her screen.

"No touching, Rip's Mom."

"Not touching," she said. "Just looking."

"That's cheating," I said. "That's violating the spirit of the rule, and you know it."

"Have you decided what you're going to name your dog, Mason Irving?" Red asked.

Mom put down her burger. "You're getting a dog?"

"No," I said. "Red and I . . . We were talking the other day and . . ." I grabbed the last fry off his plate. "Thanks a lot, Red." I popped it into my mouth. "*If* I get a dog, I'm giving it a basketball name."

"A basketball name?" Mom tonged more fries out of the bowl and dropped them onto Red's plate. "Like Shaq?"

"No!" we said at the same time.

I grabbed a handful of fries from the bowl. "Maybe I'll name it Boogie."

"Use the tongs," Mom said.

"Or Magic." I picked up a single fry with the tongs and put it in my mouth. "Like this?"

Mom glared.

"What?" I said.

"Nothing."

"If it was nothing, you wouldn't be looking at me like that."

"It's . . . it's nothing, Rip. We'll talk about it later."

"Ha!" I waved a fry. "I told you it wasn't nothing."

She faced Red. "What would you name your dog if you got one?"

"Oh, man!" Red grabbed the edge of the counter and swiveled faster. "If I got a dog . . . if I got a dog . . . that would be amazing. Amazing!"

"Slow down, Red," Mom said.

Red stopped spinning but still held on to the counter. "If I got a dog, that would be . . . that would be the best thing ever!" He bounced on his stool. "I would name her . . . I would name her when I met her. She would tell me."

"Tell you?" I poked his cheek with a fry. "You're getting a talking dog?"

"No, Mason Irving." He swatted my hand and squinched his face. "I would know when I met her."

"Her." I laughed. "Red's getting a girl dog because he's afraid a boy dog will pee all over him!"

Sleepover

I was lying on my back on my bed. The room was completely dark except for the plug-in nightlight next to the end table. I only used the nightlight when Red stayed over. He was on the air mattress on the floor.

"What do you think Mr. Acevedo would look like without hair?" Red asked.

"He'd look weird," I said.

"Mr. Acevedo would definitely look weird without hair. Will you ever cut your hair, Mason Irving?"

I pulled the locks on the top of my head forward so they hung over my eyes. Up until fourth grade, I buzzed my hair. Or I should say Mom buzzed my hair.

"At some point," I said. "I'm trying to remember what Diego looked like without hair."

"We never saw Diego Vasquez without hair. He always wore a hat."

"True, true."

"I'm glad Diego Vasquez no longer has cancer."

Cancer. I'd never heard Red say the word before. I know I never did. Not even to Mom when we were talking about Diego.

"Diego's a beast on the court," I said.

"U-N-S-T-O-P-P-A-B-L-E," Red spelled.

I laughed. "You know it."

"Just like me," Red added.

"Like you?" I propped myself up on my elbow.

"Like me, Mason Irving. That lefty pass I made to Elbows—hashtag SCtop10!"

"Dadada, dadada." I made the *SportsCenter* music.

We laughed.

"I'm going to rise to the occasion, which is life," Red said.

"You always do."

"I'm going to rise to the occasion, which is life with Clifton United."

I sat up. "How so?"

"I'm coming to the Jack Twyman Spring Showdown."

"Seriously?" I clicked on the light.

"Seriously, Mason Irving."

I tossed my purple teddy into the air, dove off my bed, and hugged Red like I'd never hugged him before.

"Boo-yah!" I shouted.

Up until this year, I never would have jumped on Red

like this. But like I said, so much about Red has changed this year. Now we'll even play-wrestle.

"Blake Daniels is coming to the Showdown!" I rolled off the air mattress and stomped my feet. "Blake Daniels is coming to the Showdown!"

"I have to come to the Jack Twyman Spring Showdown, Mason Irving."

"Why's that?"

"I told Coach Acevedo I'd be there."

"You did? When?"

"Coach Acevedo put me on notice. Coach Acevedo said if and when the time comes we need a close-out play, I was the man."

"You are the man."

"I'm your man. That's what I told Coach Acevedo. I have to be there, Mason Irving."

"Blake Daniels is coming to the Showdown! Blake Daniels is coming to the Showdown!" I swatted his shoulder. "You didn't tell me you sent Coach Acevedo a play."

"Pacer," Red said. "That was the name of the play the Valparaiso University Crusaders ran when they—"

"Why'd you choose a college play?" I interrupted. "You only watch NBA."

Red reached for the Nerf ball. "I couldn't come up with an NBA play."

"You know everything about the NBA. You couldn't come up with a play?"

"I came up with three plays."

"What was wrong with those?"

"I couldn't decide which one I liked best." Red tossed the Nerf from hand to hand. "I wanted to send Coach Acevedo the Michael Jordan play from game five of the 1989 Eastern Conference first-round series between the Chicago Bulls and the Cleveland Cavaliers. I also wanted to send Coach Acevedo the Derek Fisher play from game five of the 2004 Western Conference Finals between the Los Angeles Lakers and the San Antonio Spurs. I also wanted to send Coach Acevedo the LeBron James play from game two of the 2009 first-round series between the Cleveland Cavaliers and the Orlando Magic."

"So you chose the Pacer play instead."

"So I chose the Pacer play instead. When the thirteenth-seeded Valparaiso University Crusaders defeated the fourth-seeded University of Mississippi Rebels, it was one of the biggest upsets in the history of the NCAA tournament. The thirteen seed beat the four seed!"

"That's why they call it March Madness." I clapped for the ball.

Red tossed it to me. "That's definitely why they call it March Madness."

"Blake Daniels is coming to the Showdown!" I squeezed the Nerf. "Blake Daniels is coming to the Showdown!"

"You should watch the video of the play," Red said. "It's beautiful."

I laughed. "Beautiful?"

"Beautiful. You should watch the video."

I pulled my laptop off my workstation, and a few moments later I'd found a slow-motion YouTube clip.

As I watched, Red stood up and flipped the air mattress onto my bed.

"With two-point-five seconds left in the game," he said, "the Valparaiso University Crusaders needed to go the length of the court." He pointed to the hoop over my closet. "Jamie Sykes of the Valparaiso University Crusaders had the ball out of bounds in the corner. Jamie Sykes pump-faked and fired a perfect three-quarter-court pass to Bill Jenkins. Bill Jenkins outjumped a University of Mississippi Rebels defender for the ball." Red ran to the end of my bed and pretended to catch a pass. "Bill Jenkins tapped the ball to his teammate Bryce Drew. Bryce Drew was racing down the sideline. Bryce Drew put up a running twenty-three-footer as time expired." Red took the shot.

It bounced off the rim.

"But Bryce Drew made the basket," I said, tossing my laptop onto my pillow and scrambling after the Nerf.

"But Bryce Drew made the basket," Red said. "The Valparaiso University Crusaders practiced Pacer every day at practice, but Pacer almost never worked."

"It worked when it counted." I dunked the ball.

"It definitely worked when it counted, Mason Irving."

I pulled the air mattress back onto the floor and leaped onto my bed. "Blake Daniels is coming to the Showdown! Blake Daniels is coming to the Showdown!"

Red jumped up next to me.

"We're playing basketball." I sang the song from Xbox.

Red joined in. "We love that basketball!"

Sunday Night Bomb

I was outside on the driveway trying to spin a basketball on my finger when Mom opened the front door.

"Looking good," she said. "You're really getting the hang of it."

"You should see Diego," I said. "He can keep it going for like a minute."

"Pretty soon so will you." She walked up. "You had fun with Red?"

"He's coming to the Showdown!"

"It's wonderful, Rip. Suzanne is positively thrilled."

I swatted the spinning ball four times before it rolled off my fingertip. "Coach Acevedo is going to be pumped."

Mom held out her hands. I scooped up the ball and flipped it to her. She started spinning it on her finger.

"One day, you'll be as good as me," she said, smacking the ball and spinning it faster.

"Go, Mom!"

"I still got it," she said, smiling.

Mom played varsity basketball in high school, and up until a couple years ago, she played in a co-ed league with some of her educator friends. But she decided to stop after some of the other players started twisting ankles and tweaking muscles, trying to do things they used to do when they were younger. Mom didn't want to be next.

She handed me back the ball and picked a piece of lint out of my hair. "Honey, I hate to do this to you now," she said.

"Do what?" I got the ball going again.

"It's a Sunday Night Bomb."

What's a Sunday Night Bomb?

A Sunday Night Bomb is when you wait until eight o'clock Sunday night to tell Mom you need to bring something to the school party tomorrow, and you went with her to Trader Joe's twice over the weekend but didn't say anything either time.

A Sunday Night Bomb is when you wait until eight o'clock Sunday night to tell Mom you need a poster board for your science project and that the printer is out of ink, and you were at Staples with her that afternoon.

A Sunday Night Bomb is when you wait until eight o'clock Sunday night to tell Mom you need permission slips, waivers, and medical forms filled out for basketball, and those permission slips, waivers, and medical forms have been sitting in your gym bag for a week.

I'm the king of Sunday Night Bombs.

"Are you going to tell me?" I asked.

"Honey, your father's back in town."

This time it wasn't the ball that wobbled.

"He'd like to see you."

Detonation

"Knock, knock," Mom said, pushing open my door.

I was on my bedroom floor with my knees to my chest and my arms wrapped around my legs.

"Can I come in?"

My answer didn't matter. She sat down in the chair by my workstation and rolled closer.

"I waited to tell you because I didn't want to ruin your weekend," she said.

I pulled my legs in tighter and rocked back and forth.

"Honey, no matter when I told you, it was going to be the wrong—"

"When did you find out?"

"Tuesday. I knew he was—"

"Tuesday?"

"The day we went to Perky's."

"You waited until now to tell me?"

She reached back for the pencil by my printer. "Like I started to say, no matter when I told you—"

"I can't believe you didn't tell me."

"I probably should've told you—"

"Probably?"

"He texted while you were at practice." She strummed the pencil against her leg. "We stopped at Perky's on the way home because I wanted Dana's advice."

"You told Dana before you told me?"

"Honey, don't even. That's not what this is about, and you know it. This is about David."

I winced at the sound of his name.

My father left when I was in first grade. His company moved to the other side of the planet. He was offered a job he couldn't pass up. So he says.

When he first moved away, we Skyped or FaceTimed two or three times a week. Then it became two or three times a month. Then it became even less than that. After what happened in third grade, I didn't want to have anything to do with him.

"When?" I asked.

"When what?"

I let out a puff. "When does he want to see me?"

"He wants to see you play in the Showdown."

"No!" I banged my shoulders into the mattress behind me.

"Honey, before you—"

"No! He can't. If he's going, I'm not."

"You don't mean that."

"Yes, I do. If he's going, I'm not. I don't care."

"What about Red?"

"I don't care."

"I know you don't mean that."

"Yes, I do." I rammed my elbow into the mattress. "He can't come to the Showdown."

"Honey, this is a good way for you two to finally—"

"No!" I rammed it again.

And again.

And again.

"Rip, enough," she said firmly. *"Enough."*

I slammed it once more and let out a harder puff.

"We need to talk about this," she said.

"No, we don't." I folded my arms tightly across my chest.

"It's time we start dealing with this situation. We decided several months ago that—"

"You decided. I didn't."

Right around New Year's, Mom began making a huge deal about how this was a big year for me. I was graduating from RJE and starting middle school, and she expected to see even more growing up from me. She made a point of saying *even more* because I already was behaving more grown-up, and she knew it. But she also made a point of saying when it came to my father, I needed to stop kicking the can down the road, as she put it. She said I needed to start taking steps toward reconnecting with him.

"I'm going to be with my team," I said.

"He understands that, Rip. He wants to see you play ball and—"

"No way." I smacked the carpet.

"Honey, it's been almost two whole years since you last saw him. Who knows? You may decide you want to spend some time with him."

"No, I won't."

My brain flashed back to *The Wizard of Oz*, the RJE school play in third grade. That was the last time I saw him. The whole class were Munchkins. He was supposed to come see me in it. He got there in time to see the Wicked Witch of the West melt. He left when the cast went out for ice cream afterward.

"Was this why you were looking at me like that at dinner?" I asked.

She nodded. "But I wasn't going to say anything in front of Red." She brushed her knuckles along my cheek.

I leaned away. "I don't want him there."

"It's time we start dealing with this."

"You said that already." I smacked the carpet again. "He ruins everything."

"No, he doesn't."

"You're defending him?"

"He doesn't need to be defended, Rip. Your father and I are on the same page about this. We have been ever since we found out he was being transferred back later this year."

I let out another hard puff. "Thanks for the Sunday Night Bomb."

"I am sorry about that," she said. "Honestly, I am. But your father knows all about how much—"

"How does he know anything about me? He doesn't care about—"

"Really, Rip?" She tilted up my chin. "Who do you think pays for that cell phone of yours? And how many pairs of sneakers do you have? Three? You think I paid for those on my own? Your video games? That laptop?"

I slammed my elbows against the mattress.

Pressing Matters

For the rest of the night, I couldn't focus on anything. I couldn't read, I couldn't play Xbox, I couldn't even make it through an episode of *Teen Titans Go!*

I was only able to sleep in bursts. I kept waking up, and each time I did, I started thinking about *him*. Then it would take me forever to fall back asleep. After about the fifth or sixth time, I gave up.

School was just as frustrating. During Teacher's Theater Time, Mr. Acevedo read the next chapter of *Glory Be*, but I couldn't tell you a single thing that happened. Come to think of it, I don't even remember if he read to us in the room or the Amp. At lunch I think I sat with Red, Avery, and Attie, and at recess I'm pretty sure I played kickball.

Maybe.

I *needed* practice this afternoon. I needed basketball mode.

* * *

Basketball mode wasn't happening. Not at all.

At the beginning of practice, Maya made a huge deal of Red coming to the Showdown. She had him take a victory lap around the gym, and then when he took his free throw, she had everyone chanting, "You're the man! You're the man!"

I didn't chant. I couldn't shake *him*.

When we went over breaking the press, Coach Acevedo wanted us to share what we needed to keep in mind. A-Wu brought up spreading the floor, staying away from corners, and avoiding traps. Zoe talked about how the person inbounding the ball after a basket was allowed to run the baseline, but most defenses didn't realize it. Maya mentioned passing, how passing was faster than dribbling, and when it came to passes, you had to meet the ball, not wait for it to come to you. Diego talked about the importance of fakes—ball fakes, head fakes, bob fakes.

I didn't say anything. In my head, I was at the Showdown. I was on the court. *He* was in the bleachers. I couldn't see him, only hear him.

"Looking good, thirty-two."

"Let's see what you got, thirty-two."

"Take it to the hole, thirty-two."

Toward the end of practice, Red taught everyone his Pacer play. First, he punched up the slow-motion YouTube vid on Coach Acevedo's iPad. Then he walked Clifton United through it and made sure everyone knew all the parts.

Each time Red looked my way, hoping I'd add something, I just stood there.

Full Basketball Mode

Twenty–two hours and twenty–five minutes later...

Diego, Maya, Speedy, Red, and I huddled at the top of the key. At the other end of the court, Elbows, A-Wu, Super-Size, Zoe, and Mimi were setting their offense and getting ready to start the scrimmage.

Clifton United never scrimmaged. I could count on zero fingers the number of times we scrimmaged during fall ball, but Coach Acevedo wanted us to get in some game-style action. This was going to be our last practice before the Showdown because the gym wasn't available the rest of the week.

I pressed my thumbs and knuckles to my lips and closed my eyes. A couple minutes ago, when Coach Acevedo told me to choose my five, I was all over it. I had to be. Today was going to be different. Today *had* to be different.

"Yo, could you have picked a smaller team?" Diego said as he pulled the blue pinnie over his head.

"That's what you said the other day," I said, "and that small-ball team kicked butt." I pointed to the bench. "I can swap you out for Hudson or Mehdi, if you like."

"No way."

I flicked his ear. "That's what I thought."

Going small-ball gave Clifton United our best chance at winning. We showed that at practice last week. We were going to show it again right now.

"Who's guarding who?" Maya asked.

"I want Super-Size," I said. "Who wants A-Wu?"

"I do." Red's hand shot up. "I want Amy 'A-Wu' Wu."

"You ready?" I held out my fist.

Red gave me a pound. "Ready as I'll ever be, Mason Irving."

This was Red's first-ever full-contact scrimmage. He was in full basketball mode just like I was. Today, I was here for him. I wasn't letting my friend down again.

"We're all helping each other out," I said once we all knew who we had. "After we get a stop, we push it down-court. They're not going to be able to match up with us." I clapped hard. "Let's do this."

Tweet! Tweet!

"One thing before we start," Coach Acevedo said. "No trash talk today. I'm calling a moratorium on all the chatter, and if you don't know what *moratorium* means, look it up when you go home."

I was pretty sure I knew what *moratorium* meant. It was something we weren't allowed to do anymore.

"We're playing Clifton United basketball." Coach Acevedo backpedaled to the sideline. "Yellow ball underneath."

Usually when I'm on D, I pick up my man near midcourt, but since I had Super-Size, I was down low near the hoop. Of course Super-Size wanted to post me up, but I wasn't about to let that happen. I had one arm pressed against his back and the other extended, denying him the ball.

With my basketball eyes, I watched A-Wu set the offense. She was looking to go right to Elbows, but Red was forcing her left. I spotted Zoe sliding up from the corner and knew that's where A-Wu was heading.

It was time for the Gnat.

When I played third-grade select, the other teams called me Gnat because I was annoying on defense. Like a gnat.

I burst around Super-Size and bolted for the passing lane. I got my fingers on A-Wu's pass and tipped it enough so that Zoe couldn't catch it cleanly. Red snatched the ball away.

"Blake Daniels with the steal!" I announced. "He flips it to Diego, who pushes it up. Diego dishes to Speedy in the paint. Speedy kicks it out to Irving. Irving whips it to Maya. Oh, what a pass! Cutting down the lane . . . the layup . . . It's good! Everyone was in on that one. Oh, what a play!"

Tweet! Tweet!

"That was a thing of beauty!" Coach Acevedo bounded onto the court and gave pounds all around. "At both ends of the floor, a thing of beauty." He pointed his whistle at me. "That's the Rip I want to see! Way to make everyone around you better."

I smiled big.

"Yo, that was real Rip Hamilton basketball!" Diego tapped the back of my head.

"Next level," I said, thumping my chest. "Now let's get the ball to Red this time."

Once again, I matched up with Super-Size in the paint, and once again, A-Wu passed to Elbows. But this time, as soon as he caught it, Maya moved in for the steal. Elbows tried to dribble around her, but Speedy slid over to help, and Elbows stepped out of bounds.

Tweet! Tweet!

"Blue ball on the side," Coach Acevedo called.

It was time to make everyone around me better again.

I dribbled up the floor and passed to Maya. She looked inside and swung the ball back to me. I was about to reverse it to Red when I spotted Diego sprinting into the lane. I fired the ball his way. He caught it and faced the hoop. He had a clean shot, but he also had Red wide open cutting to the basket. Diego hit him in stride. Red sank the layup.

"Boo-yah!" I hammer-fisted the air.

"Bam!" Red jumped up and down. He double-fist-bumped Diego. "Bam!" Then he double-fist-bumped Maya and Speedy. "Bam! Bam!" He spun to me. "Bam, Mason Irving!"

Hoodie Time

"Thursday's meeting here at RJE starts at six-thirty sharp," Coach Acevedo said when we circled up by the stage at the end of practice. "It won't be a long meeting, but it is mandatory. Everyone needs to be here with a parent or guardian. I'll send out all the deets in an email this evening."

"Will there be food?" Diego asked.

"Yes, Diego, there will be food," Coach Acevedo said.

"Sweet!" Diego drum-rolled the floor. "I'm so there."

"It also looks like we resolved our chaperone dilemma," Coach Acevedo added. "I'll know for sure in the next day or so. I'll keep you posted." He held up a finger. "Give me a sec. I have something for everyone." He headed for the sideline.

"Sick cut on that pass from Diego," I said, tapping Red's knee. He was sitting beside me on the front of the stage.

"Thanks, Mason Irving."

"That was the best I've ever seen you play."

"That makes two of us," Maya added. She was on the other side of Red.

"Thanks, Maya Wade." Red basketball-smiled and swung his legs.

"So I have something for you," Coach Acevedo said, jogging back over with a large carton. "A surprise."

"A good surprise?" Maya asked. She slid off the stage.

"I think so." He put the carton down and opened the top flaps. "There's one for everyone. They're all the same size."

Speedy reached the box first and pulled out a folded navy Clifton United hoodie.

"Sweet!" Diego knee-slid to the box and grabbed three. He tossed one to Hudson and one to Maya.

"These are hot!" Speedy said, shaking out her sweatshirt and holding it up.

"Ballin'!" Maya said. She put hers on.

Diego handed out the rest.

"Oh, yeah!" Red said when he got his. He jumped off the stage. "Thanks, Coach Acevedo."

"Don't thank me," he said. "Thank Mehdi's dad the next time you see him. He's the one who had them made."

Elbows high-fived Mehdi. Zoe and Super-Size gave him pounds.

"Yo, we should all wear these on Friday," Diego said, putting his on.

"I like that," Coach Acevedo said. "I'll include a reminder in the email."

"I feel like I'm wearing a hospital gown again," Diego said, leaping onto the stage. His hoodie was a little big on him. "Can I tell my hospital gown story?" He looked at Coach Acevedo.

"Do we have a choice?"

Diego flipped up his hood and swatted the strings. "The first few times I was in the hospital, I had to wear a gown.

But I always forgot to tie it, and my beautiful butt would always hang out." He turned around, lifted up the sweat-shirt, and shook his butt. "So my uncle made me a glitter 'Kick Me' sign and clipped it to the back of my gown. I wore it everywhere!"

"Thanks, Diego," Coach Acevedo said.

"Can I say one more thing?" Diego jumped off the stage and held up his hand like he was taking an oath. "I promise it's not about my beautiful butt."

Coach Acevedo motioned for him to go ahead.

"When you're in the hospital for as long as I was," Diego said, "you start to wonder if you're ever going to get out. You can't help it." He swallowed. "So I just wanted to say thanks . . . because one of the things . . . one of the things that kept me going was the thought of playing on a basket-ball team with my friends. Like this." He thumped his chest. "Clifton United rocks."

kids in the Hall

Zoe, Diego, and I sat on the polka-dotted beanbag chairs facing Red, Mehdi, and Speedy, who were on the denim couch. The rest of Clifton United sat on the floor around the pizza boxes.

We'd dragged the furniture out of Room 208 and down the hall when Coach Acevedo said the kids could leave the meeting. That was right after the pizza arrived, which was right after we learned our hotel room assignments.

I was rooming with Red, Diego, and Elbows. The three other boys—Hudson, Mehdi, and Super-Size—were in the connecting room with Coach Acevedo. The five girls and Ms. Yvonne were sharing connecting rooms, too. The third chaperone was staying in a separate room, which seemed kind of odd.

"Yo, you two better not fart in your sleep," Diego said, pointing his pizza crust at Red and me.

Red squinched his face. "I don't fart in my sleep, Diego Vasquez."

"I do!" Super-Size raised his water bottle. "Juicy farts! Loud, juicy—"

"Do you mind?" Maya said. "I'm eating."

"My dog farts in his sleep," Hudson said.

Everyone laughed.

"He does." Hudson nodded. "He's a puny little pug, but I swear, his farts can clear a room."

Everyone laughed again.

I checked Red. He was eating his pizza the way he always ate pizza. Peeling the toppings off the crust. Eating the toppings. Eating the cheese. Licking off the sauce. Not eating the crust. Red never ate the crust. He always gave the crust to me.

I eat everything.

"Do any of you girls toot in your sleep?" Diego asked.

"Gross!" Zoe shook her hands by her face.

"I'm just asking," Diego said, grinning. "Don't you want to know if your roommates toot in their sleep? I wonder if Ms. Yvonne toots in—"

A piece of pepperoni hit his cheek and fell onto his shirt.

"Oh!" a bunch of us said.

"There's more where that came from," Maya said, pointing to her slice.

Diego flicked off the pepperoni. "Yo, that's exactly why I didn't wear my hoodie," he said.

Most of us had worn our hoodies. It looked pretty cool seeing everyone wearing them. We were going to look hot walking into the Showdown dressed in Clifton United swag.

"I still need to thank your dad for the sweatshirts," A-Wu said to Mehdi.

"Me too," said Hudson.

"It wasn't just my dad," Mehdi said. "It was my mom, too. Mostly my mom. My dad came up with the idea. My mom designed and ordered them."

"So what's the deal with Elbows?" Mimi asked.

"That's what I want to know," Speedy said.

I wanted to know, too. Elbows didn't come tonight, and tonight was mandatory. When Coach Acevedo said something was mandatory, he meant it.

"Yo, it's messed up he isn't here," Diego said.

"Was he in school?" Speedy asked Super-Size.

"Yeah," Super-Size said, "but he didn't say anything about not coming. He'd better come to the Showdown."

"You're telling me." I rolled off the beanbag chair to the pizza and grabbed another slice. "A little better than RJE cafeteria pizza, right?" I said to Diego.

"Yo, that pizza box tastes better than our school pizza."

"Our school pizza is ballin'," Maya disagreed. "It's better than pizzeria pizza."

Coach Acevedo popped his head into the hall. "About ten more minutes," he said, holding up his hands. "Everyone's good down here?"

"We're good," Super-Size said.

We all laughed. For no reason. We just did. Fifth graders do that sometimes.

"Make sure you save me a couple slices," Coach Acevedo added. Then he ducked back into the room.

"I wish we had a couch and beanbag chairs in our classroom," Zoe said. "All we have are desks and chairs."

"We have to sit in rows," Hudson said. "Assigned seats."

"We sit wherever we want, Hudson Moss," Red said. "I mean . . . not wherever we want." He put down what was left of his pizza and shook his fingers by his face. "We can't move around, but we . . . we choose where we want to sit. This month, I'm sitting with Trinity Webster, Attie Silverman, and Mason Irving."

"Dag, I almost forgot." I popped to my feet. "Back in a sec."

I ran down the hall to Room 208. When I reached the door, I stopped dead in my tracks. It looked so weird seeing all the grown-ups sitting in *our* seats. Suzanne and Mom were at *my* table.

"Hey, everyone," I said, waving.

"What can I do for you?" Coach Acevedo asked.

I pointed to the book bin on the windowsill. "Need *True Believer*," I said.

I quick-walked across the room, love-tapped Mom on the shoulder, and grabbed the book.

"Nothing to see here, everyone," I said, heading back to the door. "Nothing at all."

A few parents laughed.

I scooted out and sprinted down the hallway. "That's my seat," I said to A-Wu, who'd snagged my beanbag chair.

"You didn't call fives," she said.

"I'll remember that." I sat down on the floor and held up the book. "Coach Acevedo got me a copy of *True Believer* from the middle school library."

"What's *True Believer*?" Zoe asked.

I tapped the cover. "This is where our team mantra comes from."

"We will rise to the occasion, which is life," Diego said. He stood on the beanbag chair and jumped in circles. "We will rise to the occasion! We will rise to the occasion!"

I grabbed the back of his shirt and pulled him down. "The character that says it is one of the teachers," I said, opening to the page with the blue stickie. "Her name is Dr. Rose."

"Are you going to read to us, Ripster?" Diego said, baby-talking.

That's exactly what I was planning on doing. I was going to read the passage from the book. But now, all of a sudden, that idea seemed mad corny.

"We will rise to the occasion, which is life," Red said, standing up. "We will rise to the occasion, which is life."

I smiled. Sometimes Red did the coolest things in the

world without even realizing he was doing the coolest things in the world.

I stood up. "We will rise to the occasion, which is life," I said.

Then everyone else stood. "We will rise to the occasion, which is life!"

Thursday Night Bomb

On the way home from the meeting, Mom and I went by Stop 'n Save. Mom likes to do her big food shopping on weeknights because the store usually isn't as crowded as it is on weekends. She lets me push the cart now that I've learned not to bump into the backs of people's legs (people *really* don't like that) or knock over the display of spaghetti sauce (it only happened once).

I followed her into the produce section.

"You're having corn on the cob without me?" I said, hopping onto the cart's underbar and rolling up to the fresh sweet corn, this week's manager's special, according to the sign.

"Sure looks that way," she said, dropping a few ears into the cart.

"That's cold, Mom."

Corn on the cob was our absolute fave. There's nothing better than fresh, sweet corn on the cob off the grill.

"Maybe we'll have some with dinner after you're back on Sunday."

"Maybe?"

She smiled. "I can't guarantee there'll be any left." She pointed up the aisle. "Grab a couple baskets of strawberries. Just make sure the label says organic. Sometimes they inadvertently mix in toxic ones."

Toxic. That's what Mom calls fresh fruits and vegetables that aren't organic.

"Why were you texting during the meeting?" I asked. I was still standing on the cart's underbar.

"You saw that?"

"Yeah, I saw. *You* were texting."

Mom's never the person who texts when someone's talking. She doesn't even like it when people tweet out what she's saying at a workshop or meeting. She likes to be able to see people's eyes. She likes everyone to be present.

"I was putting out a fire at school," Mom said. "I told Coach Acevedo ahead of time I would be using my phone. I didn't want him to think I was being rude."

I pressed my chest to the cart handle, kicked out my feet, and jumped off. I air-dribbled like Iverson to the strawberries, grabbed a couple nontoxic cartons, and stacked them next to the corn on the cob that had no chance of making it to Sunday.

"There was another reason why I was texting," Mom said. "That's what we need to talk about."

"I don't like the way that sounds."

She pulled a plastic bag from the dispenser. "It has to do with your father."

"I told you I didn't like the way that sounded."

"Honey, I—"

"Do we have to talk about it here?"

"You leave for the Showdown tomorrow, Rip. When else are we going to?"

"How about never?"

She pointed to the fruit behind me. "Nectarines, peaches, or plums?"

"Peaches," I said. "No, make that plums."

"I didn't want to bring it up until I knew for absolute certain." She stepped around the cart to the red plums. "Your father won't be getting to the Showdown until Saturday morning."

"I bet he doesn't even show."

"He'll show." She nodded to the red onions. "Will you grab a four-pound bag? That's the bigger bag."

"I still don't think he's my real father."

"We're not having *that* conversation," she said firmly. "You know how much—"

"He looks nothing like me," I said anyway. I flipped the

mesh bag of onions into the cart. "I bet if he took one of those paternity—"

She cut me off. "I said, we're *not* having that conversation. Even though your father and I weren't together all that long, we—"

"Long enough." I held my arms out wide.

"Yes, long enough. And there was no one else. That's how I know he's your father. There hasn't been anyone else either."

"You've been with Dana."

"Well, Dana and I don't exactly have the necessary equipment."

I covered my ears. "Overshare!"

"You brought it up." She placed her hands atop mine on the handle. "Rip, you're not making this any easier for me right now. Let me just say this."

"Say what?"

She paused. "When your father gets there Saturday morning, he's going to be the third chaperone."

"No he's not!" I tried sliding my hands out from under hers, but she held my fingers.

"He is, Rip. It's the only—"

"He's not!"

"Coach Acevedo wasn't able to secure a third chaperone. This was the only solution."

"Only?" I slammed my foot into the display behind me. "This is so not fair!"

She squeezed my fingers. "Honey, your father is saving the Showdown for the team."

"How can you do this to me?" I kicked the display again.

"Without your father, Clifton United can't go."

All Night Long

9:45

I lay on my bed and stared at the ceiling.

I knew it'd sounded weird when Coach Acevedo said the third chaperone was staying in a separate room. I knew it. I was right.

How can he do this to me?

I clicked off the light.

* * *

11:16

I'm not going. No way.

I smacked the wall next to my bed.

"No!"

I don't care that Red needs me there. Why does everything always have to be about Red? This isn't about Red.

I smacked the wall again.

* * *

12:22

Coach Acevedo's words played on a loop in my head.

We're counting on you big-time, Rip. We need you to pick up where you left off at the end of fall ball. You're Clifton United's floor leader, our team general. I'm going to be pushing you hard, real hard.

I covered my ears.

* * *

1:30

He was getting there on Saturday, but I didn't know when. I had to be ready. I clasped my hands, pressed my thumbs and knuckles to my lips, and played out the scenes. Pictured them, visualized them. Like I did for hoops. So that when it happened for real, I'd already seen it.

He's there when the bus pulls up to Hoops Haven. Leaning against the sign in front. Wearing faded jeans, an untucked long-sleeve white button-down, and red low-top Converse. The same outfit he wore to The Wizard of Oz.

He shows up when we're eating breakfast at the hotel. He sits down in a booth by the window. He smiles and waves me over. Everyone sees him smile and wave me over.

He gets there during the first quarter. He doesn't sit in the bleachers. He stands beyond the baseline. Under the basket. Barking at the referee.

I had to be ready. So that when it happened for real, I'd already seen it.

* * *

2:04

I sat on my bedroom floor with my writer's notebook in my lap. The page was still blank. We were allowed to write whatever we wanted, and if we didn't want Mr. Acevedo to read what we wrote, all we had to do was turn down the top corner and write "DNR" on the flap.

DNR=Do Not Read.

"Writing helps my head," Mr. Acevedo liked to say. "When I'm trying to work through something or figure something out, I'll write down my thoughts. Everything that comes to mind. Sometimes just seeing the words on the page helps."

I'd never done a DNR journal entry.

* * *

2:47

DNR

How do you choose your job over your family? How do you just leave your family? You didn't have to go. No one made you go. You went on your own.

I don't know what to write but I know I have to write because if I don't write something I'm going to explode. This riuns everything. You left. You left me. You left us. Now you want to come back and watch me play and think your part of the team. I don't want you here. I don't want to see you. I don't want to see you ever, ever, ever!

* * *

3:08

We have to start dealing with this. That's what she says. I have to stop kicking the can down the road. I have to start taking steps toward reconnecting with him.

Who do you think pays for that cell phone of yours? And how many pairs of sneakers do you have? Three? You think I paid for those on my own? Your video games? That laptop?

I held my purple teddy by the arms and chewed on the ear.

Your father and I are on the same page about this. We have been ever since we found out he was being transferred back later this year.

* * *

3:58

I told Red he had to come to the Showdown. I told him he couldn't miss it. I told him it wouldn't be the same without him. I told him everyone wanted him there. I told him it was going to be sick.

I gripped the back of my neck with one hand and squeezed purple teddy's belly with the other.

Zombie-Walking

A few hours later, Red and I walked to school like we do every morning. Only this morning wasn't like every other morning.

As we headed down Orleans Lane, Red kept looking over. He wanted to talk, but I hadn't said a word yet, and the longer I stayed silent, the faster he patted his fists against his legs.

I was the one who always started our walking-to-school conversations. It wasn't like a rule or anything. That's just the way it was. But not today.

Today, I was zombie-walking.

I blinked hard. My head was in such a haze. I'd slept an hour last night. Maybe. When Mom came in to wake me, I was on the floor. No pillow, no covers, just me and purple teddy.

We turned onto Key Place.

"You're thinking about that thing again," Red said.

"What thing?"

"He speaks!" The words exploded from Red's mouth.

"Ha." I managed a small smile. "How long have you been waiting to say that line?"

"Since my driveway, Mason Irving."

I was barely able to see what was in front of me and was shuffling along like I do after finishing my last set of end-of-practice up-and-backs, but it still registered that Red had made a joke. Not a joke-joke, but a funny comment. Red used to never say things like that.

"You're thinking about that thing again," he repeated. "You were thinking about it on the walk to school on Monday. You were thinking about it in—"

"No I'm not."

"Yes you are, Mason Irving. Something's up."

Red always knows when something's up, and most of the time he knows exactly what that something is.

I let out a puff. "It's not . . . Well, there's more to it now."

"Why don't you want to go to the Jack Twyman Spring Showdown?" he asked.

I flinched. "What?"

"Why don't you want to go to the Jack Twyman Spring Showdown?"

"Who says I don't want to go?"

"You did."

"When did I say that?"

"Right now. You're saying it right now, Mason Irving."

Like I said, Red knows when something's up and, most of the time, exactly what that something is.

"Why don't you want your father to be a chaperone?" Red asked.

I didn't even know Red knew my father was the third chaperone, but it made sense that he did because everyone's gotten a lot better about letting him know about unexpected changes and surprises.

"I don't really remember your father," he said.

"Not much to remember."

"Does your father know basketball? If your father knows basketball, maybe—"

"Can we not talk about him?"

He turtled his neck. "Sorry, Mason Irving."

We turned onto Niagara Drive. Red spun around the stop sign at the corner.

"You have to be there, Mason Irving," Red said. "You can't miss this. You know you want to go."

That's what I'd said to Red. Pretty much word-for-word. He was right. I had to be there. No matter how badly I didn't want to go, no matter how badly I didn't want to see him, I had to be there.

"I know," I said softly. "I'm going."

"Yes!" Red said. "We're going to the Jack Twyman Spring Showdown." He started skip-walking. "The Hoops Haven Sports Complex is supposed to be amazing."

"The hotel has an indoor pool," I said.

"My mom packed my goggles," Red said. "She packed a pair for you, too."

"I'll wear them."

Whenever Red goes swimming, he always wears goggles. He won't go in the water without them because he doesn't like getting splashed in the face or getting chlorine in his eyes. He also doesn't like being the only kid wearing goggles. So I wear them, too.

"I'll make sure no one splashes you," I said. I bumped his shoulder. "I'll get you a noodle."

"No!"

"Why not?"

"I don't need a noodle." He hunched his shoulders. "I can swim. I've been taking swim lessons with Coach Lisa since kindergarten. I've been taking—"

"Noodles are the best," I said. "I'll take yours if you don't want one."

"Steph Curry's taking my noodle."

"Huh?"

"Maybe Steph Curry will be at the pool." Red smiled. "Maybe Steph Curry will be at the pool because he heard that Clifton United's U-N-S-T-O-P-P-A-B-L-E point guard is going to be there." He laughed.

I laughed, too. Red made another joke. A joke-joke that was funny.

We turned into the schoolyard.

"Can I ask you something?" I said.

"Sure, Mason Irving."

"Do you ever wonder what it would be like if your dad lived with you?"

"I never met my dad," Red said.

"I know, but do you ever wonder what it would be like?"

"No."

"No?"

"No, Mason Irving."

For a few seconds, neither of us said anything. Finally, I bumped his shoulder again.

"Clifton United's going to kick butt at the Showdown," I said.

"Oh, yeah! Clifton United's definitely going to kick butt at the Jack Twyman Spring Showdown."

"How cool would it be if we won the whole thing?"

"Oh, man!" Red was skip-walking again. "If Clifton United won the Jack Twyman Spring Showdown, that would be amazing!"

I pointed to the jungle gym. Every morning on our way to school, Red and I obstacle-coursed the jungle gym. It was our favorite part of the walk to school.

"You ready?" I said.

"Ready as I'll ever be, Mason Irving."

At the Bus

As soon as the substitute teacher dismissed the class at the end of the day, Diego, Red, and I headed straight for the Clifton United team bus in the faculty lot.

We had a sub today because Mr. Acevedo had to attend an all-day staff development. He'd told the class about it yesterday, but with everything else going on inside my head, I had forgotten.

When we got to the lot, Super-Size, Mehdi, Mimi, Hudson, and Speedy were already waiting with Ms. Yvonne. Red and Diego joined them by the bus. I sat down on the curb.

Having a sub today saved me. I was able to nod off a few times during class without getting busted. It also saved me from having to interact with Mr. Acevedo. I wasn't looking forward to that. Make that, I was dreading it. He was going to take one look at me and know just how much the situation with my father was eating at me.

"Yo, the bus is sweet," Diego said, spinning a basketball on his finger. "We got to put our bags on already."

The bus had arrived at RJE while we were at recess and parked in the front circle. Principal Darling had to tell the driver to move it to the staff lot because the after-school car pickup line was in the front circle and parents would freak if a mega-bus was parked there during Thunder Dome.

That's where Mr. Acevedo was now. Thunder Dome duty. We were leaving for the Showdown as soon as he was done.

"My first away tournament," Speedy said, "and we're traveling in style!"

"We're going to the Showdown!" Mimi gave pounds all around. "Get pumped, Clifton United."

"Get pumped, Clifton United!" Red said.

I pressed my palms to my temples. I wanted to be fired up like everyone else, but I was running on fumes, and at any moment I was going to have to face Coach Acevedo.

An SUV pulled into the lot.

"Maya Wade is here!" Red said, pointing and hopping from foot to foot. "Amy 'A-Wu' Wu is here. Zoe Reynolds is here."

I half smiled. You can't help but smile seeing how happy and excited Red gets when he spots someone he knows.

"The ladies have arrived!" Maya said as she and the other two girls got out of the car. "Let's get this party started!"

Like everyone else, they were wearing their Clifton United hoodies. We were going to look hot walking into Hoops Haven.

"Elbows isn't with you?" Speedy said to the kids who'd just arrived.

"No," A-Wu answered. "Was he supposed to come with us?"

"Yo, it's messed up that he isn't here," Diego said.

I kicked out my legs and grabbed my toes. Diego was right. It was messed up. How could Elbows disappear like this? Maybe he was at Thunder Dome with Coach Acevedo. Or maybe he was meeting us at the Showdown.

"He'd better show," Maya said.

"If he doesn't," Diego said, pounding his basketball, "I'll be stepping up."

"That makes two of us," Mimi said.

"We'll all step up," Super-Size said.

"Check this out," Maya said, pulling up the front of her hoodie. "I'm representing Clifton United twice."

Underneath her sweatshirt, she was wearing a "Bench Mob" T-shirt. During fall ball, Avery from class had made shirts for the whole team.

"I'm representing!" Red said, lifting up his sweatshirt and showing off the number twenty-four Rick Barry jersey he had on under his hoodie. "I'm representing the Golden State Warriors. I'm representing Clifton United. I'm representing—"

"Let's circle up!" Coach Acevedo walked out the side entrance.

He wasn't alone. A kid in a Clifton United hoodie was with him. But it wasn't Elbows.

The New Teammate

"I want to introduce you to someone," Coach Acevedo said. We huddled by the bus. "This here is Charlie Roth. He'll be taking Elbows's place on Clifton United."

"What happened to Elbows?" Maya asked.

"Elbows isn't allowed to play for Clifton United this weekend," Coach Acevedo answered flatly. "Charlie here played on Millwood with Super-Size," Coach Acevedo said. "Most of you know him as Mega-Man. We'll be calling him that, too."

Mega-Man gave a quick wave.

I grabbed the locks above my neck and checked Super-Size. He had his arms folded across his chest and a blank look on his face.

Mega-Man was the kid who'd knocked out Keith Krebs during fall ball. He was the kid whose own teammates didn't like to hang with. He was Coach Crazy's son. In my head, when I looked at him, I saw Coach Crazy stalking the sidelines, screaming at his players, and arguing with the refs. I saw Red sitting on the end of our bench, hunched over with his fists shaking in front of his eyes.

"Mega-Man is one of us now," Coach Acevedo said, patting his shoulder. "Let's make him feel part of Clifton United."

"Welcome to Clifton United," Ms. Yvonne said.

"Welcome to Clifton United, Charlie 'Mega-Man' Roth." Red stepped forward and gave him a pound.

"Thanks, Red," Coach Acevedo said.

Maya gave him a pound, too. Then some of the others did.

I didn't. I flipped up my hood and squeezed my head with my arms. Mega-Man was on Clifton United? Why did Coach Acevedo pick Mega-Man?

"As I'm sure most of you know by now," Coach Acevedo said, "we did resolve our chaperone situation. Rip's father graciously offered to step in. He'll be meeting us at the Showdown tomorrow morning."

A few kids clapped. Diego patted my back.

I dug my hands into the pouch pocket of my hoodie and clenched my fists. Elbows wasn't coming, Mega-Man was taking his place, and my father was the third chaperone. The best basketball weekend of my life was turning into a disaster!

"When we get on the bus," Coach Acevedo said, "I'd like for someone to take Mega-Man around and introduce him to everyone."

Red's hand shot up first.

"You're the man, Red," Coach Acevedo said.

"I'm your man, Coach Acevedo."

"Yo, do you know our team mantra?" Diego asked Mega-Man.

He shook his head.

"We will rise to the occasion, which is life!" Diego leaped into the middle of the circle and did a jumping three-sixty. "We will rise to the occasion, which is life!"

Most of the kids laughed.

Suddenly, it hit me. Mega-Man was going to be rooming with us. He was going to be in the same hotel room as Diego, Red, and me. Red was going to bug. Had Coach Acevedo thought about this? How was he planning to tell Red? What if Red couldn't . . .

"Charlie 'Mega-Man' Roth can be in our hotel room," Red said, hopping. "Charlie 'Mega-Man' Roth can take Bomani 'Elbows' Taylor's place in our hotel room."

"Sounds good to me," Coach Acevedo said.

I let out a puff. So much for Red buggin'. What did I know anymore?

"You know what would sound good to me?" Diego said,

bouncing. "If Coach Acevedo said it was time to go to the Showdown."

"I'm incredibly proud of each and every one of you," Coach Acevedo said, drawing a circle in the air with his finger. "At this tournament of champions, you already are the champions." He patted the bus. "Let's go to the Showdown!"

The United Express

I pressed my head against the window and closed my eyes. My mind went back to Stop 'n Save. I was pushing the cart around the produce section, grabbing the strawberries and onions, listening to Mom.

Coach Acevedo wasn't able to secure a third chaperone. This was the only solution.

"Cannonball contest!" Diego shouted. His words jolted me back.

"Chicken fights!" Zoe said.

"Yo, even better!" Diego said. "Chicken fights! I'm with Super-Size!"

"I'm with Mimi," Speedy called.

"I'm with Maya Wade!" Red said.

The bus was big enough for everyone to have their own seat, but most of the kids were in the last two rows. Coach Acevedo had just walked back to tell everyone there would be time for a team swim before dinner.

"The pool has a basketball hoop," Hudson said.

"How do you know?" Zoe asked.

"My dad and I checked the hotel website last night," he said.

"Ballin'," Maya said.

I wasn't sitting with the others. I was toward the front of the bus. Like I had been the whole ride. We'd been on the road for about an hour.

I closed my eyes again. My brain went right back to the supermarket: Mom placing her hands on top of mine, holding my fingers, squeezing my fingers, telling me that my father—who I hadn't seen in two years and who I had no interest in ever seeing again—was chaperoning my basketball team's trip.

"Yo, you joining us?" Diego knocked on my head. He stood on the seat next to me. "It's mad fun back there. You're missing out."

I blinked hard. "In a little bit," I said.

"C'mon, Rip. It's the Showdown." Diego swatted my shoulder. "Whatever this thing with your father is, forget about it. Come back there."

"I will. Just give me a—"

"Yo, you two should be a team for chicken fights," Diego said, cutting me off. He elbow-pointed to Mega-Man diagonally across the aisle.

"Okay," I said softly.

"I will destroy you in a chicken fight, puny man!" Diego said in a weird accent. He knocked my head again, jumped off the seat, and raced back.

I looked over at Mega-Man. He was plugged in and sitting by himself. Just like he had been ever since Red finished introducing him to everyone, which took all of about three minutes because Red's not exactly the greatest conversation starter and Mega-Man wasn't exactly talkative.

I flipped up my hood, lay across both seats, and curled into a ball. I should have helped Red with the intros. Coach Acevedo and Ms. Yvonne wanted me to. They both kept looking over at me when Red was taking Mega-Man around, but I only wanted to sleep.

"Our team bus needs a name," Maya said.

"The United Mobile," Hudson said.

"The Showdown Express," Super-Size said.

"The United Express!" Diego said.

"Ballin'," Maya said. "The United Express."

"The United Express!" Red said.

I could hear his basketball smile. I don't have to be looking at Red to know when he's basketball-smiling.

My brain went back to my bedroom. I was on the floor, chewing on purple teddy's ear, staring at the journal in my lap.

How do you choose your job over your family? How do you just leave your family? You didn't have to go. No one made you go. You went on your own.

I shot up. I reached across the aisle and tapped Mega-Man's armrest. "What are you listening to?" I asked.

He pulled out a bud. "What?"

I pointed to his screen. "What are you listening to?"

"Just some music."

No, I thought you were listening to barking dogs and mooing cows. I gripped my neck.

"What type?"

"Just a playlist I made."

What's it like having Coach Crazy for a father? Does he act like that at home? Did that ref press charges?

"Have you ever played in a tournament?" I asked instead.

"What?" Mega-Man pulled out the earbud he'd already put back in.

"Have you ever gone on a trip like this?"

"I go camping every summer."

"That's a good book." I motioned to *Unidentified Suburban Object* on the seat next to him.

He nodded. "Yeah."

"What do you think . . . ? Never mind." I slid back over to my seat and pressed my head against the window.

* * *

"You coming?" Diego knocked my head.

"Huh?"

"Wake up, man," Diego said. "We're here."

"Whoa."

He pointed to the front of my sweatshirt and laughed. "Yo, you drooled in your sleep!"

I'd slept. The whole rest of the way, I'd slept. I smacked

the side of my head and looked around. Everyone else had gotten off the bus already. Except for Coach Acevedo, who stood in the aisle up front. He gave Diego a pound as he leaped around the front seat and down the stairs. Then he waved me forward.

I wiped the front of my hoodie with my palm and shuffled up.

"Good nap?" he said.

"I think so," I said, rubbing my eyes. "I didn't think I'd fall asleep like that."

Coach Acevedo tapped his iPad. "Losing Elbows is a tough blow."

"Why isn't he allowed to play?"

"His mother said he didn't do his schoolwork."

"Was there . . . ? Did you try talking to her?"

"I talked to Elbows," Coach Acevedo said. "He knows he let everyone down." He touched my arm. "I'm looking forward to meeting your father tomorrow. He'll be waiting for us at Hoops Haven in the morning."

I dipped my hands into my hoodie pouch and nodded.

"We Skyped for a while on Wednesday," Coach Acevedo said. "He seems like a fascinating guy."

"Okay."

"He's saving Clifton United, that's for sure." Coach Acevedo adjusted a hoop in the top of his ear. "The district insisted we have three adults present at the games. Your father's coming through big-time for us."

"Big-time," I said softly. I clenched my hidden fists.

"When we're at the pool now, try to get Mega-Man involved. Really make him feel like he's part of Clifton United."

"I will."

"I'm counting on you, Rip. You know that."

"I know."

"I did speak to your mom." He placed a hand on my shoulder. "She told me a little about the situation with your father. Not a lot, but enough to—"

"It's fine," I interrupted.

"Good," he said. "That's what I want to hear. That's what leadership's all about. Clifton United needs you focused."

Inside my pouch pocket, I pressed my knuckles together.

"We come committed," Coach Acevedo said. "No distractions. Time to rise to the occasion."

Pool Play

"**No goaltending,**" I said. I pointed to the basket by the side of the pool with the rubber ball and waved my teammates out of the way. "I'm serious, no goaltending."

"Just shoot it," Zoe said.

I adjusted my goggles. I wasn't getting a clean shot. No way. Zoe, Speedy, and Super-Size were already moving closer to the hoop, and Super-Size was waving his noodle.

I ran toward the pool, leaped into the air, and fired the ball down at the rim.

Splash!

I popped out of the water and shook my hair.

"You missed," Speedy said.

"That was *so* going in," I said.

"No way." Super-Size swatted me with his noodle.

Hudson and Diego scrambled out of the pool and chased after the ball bounding toward the lounge chairs in the corner. Diego got to it first.

We were the only ones in the pool. Coach Acevedo was letting us stay in until he and Ms. Yvonne finished filling out forms for the Showdown. They were in the lobby area watching us through the windows.

"Incoming!" Diego shouted, sprinting back to the pool. He ran off the diving board toward the hoop. "Boom! In your face!" He two-handed tomahawk-slammed the ball.

Splash!

I headed for Red and Maya in the shallow end. They were floating on their backs with noodles tucked under their arms.

"'I don't need a noodle to swim,'" I said teasingly to Red.

He squinched his face under his goggles.

"Told you you'd want one." I turned to Maya and smiled. "You should have heard Red this morning. He was whining all about how he didn't need—"

"I wasn't whining, Mason Irving," Red said.

Maya dropped to her knees and blew bubbles on the surface. "You were whining, Red?"

"No."

"Yes." I reached for a noodle, tapped the water with it, and teased him more. "'I've been taking swim lessons with Coach Lisa since kindergarten,'" I mimicked.

"Very funny," Red said.

I reached out to ruffle his hair, but he ducked away.

Then he reached for mine and got in a good shake. A little water sprayed his face, but he didn't even flinch.

I glanced over at Mehdi and Mega-Man sitting on the lounge chairs near the entrance. They were the only two who didn't come in. Mehdi didn't because he was getting over an ear infection. Mega-Man didn't because he didn't want to. I'd tried to convince him—especially since I knew how much Coach Acevedo wanted Mega-Man included—but I couldn't.

"Cannonball time!" Diego shouted. He stood in back of the diving board while we cleared a landing zone. Then he raced onto the board and sprang off. "Look out below!"

In midair, Diego wrapped his arms around his legs in cannonball position, but he hit the water more on his back than on his butt.

Splash!

"Boom! In your face!" Super-Size yelled. He scooped up the ball and held it over his head.

Diego popped out of the water and grabbed a noodle. He pointed it at Super-Size like a light saber. "Kill the giant!" he shouted, and lunged at him.

Suddenly, Mimi, Hudson, and A-Wu pounced on Super-Size. A-Wu knocked the ball out of his hands. Speedy grabbed it and threw it toward the shallow end. Maya got to it first.

"Let Red take a shot," I said.

Maya tossed him the ball. "Dial it up from long distance," she said.

"It's like your Valpo play," I said, adjusting the straps of my goggles.

"No, it's not, Mason Irving. I'm not passing the ball. In the Valparaiso University Crusaders—"

"Take your shot."

"Oh, man." Red sized up the rim.

"Two-point-five seconds left on the clock," I play-by-played. "Blake Daniels will need to go the length of the pool. He'll need a full-court miracle. Daniels launches the shot . . . It's got a chance . . ."

"Bam!" Hudson leaped into the air and punched the ball out of the pool. It bounced past Mehdi's lounge chair toward the door to the pool area just as it was opening.

Another team walked in.

Well, it looked like another team. It was a group of kids about our age, and since other teams were staying at our hotel, I figured that's who they were. It was a team of all boys. They all wore bathing suits and had blue towels. Most of them had the towels wrapped around their necks; two of the kids were wearing them like they'd just gotten out of the shower. They all had on flip-flops—some the kind you got at the dollar store, some the fly kind with white stripes and logos. One kid had on orange Houston Rockets socks.

"What's up?" said one of the kids wearing the dollar-store flip-flops. He walked to the edge of the pool and flashed a Red-like smile.

Diego held up his fist. "I'm Diego."

"Don't pull me in." He gave Diego a pound. "I'm Kasaan."

"We're Clifton United." Diego swatted the side of the pool with his noodle.

Kasaan motioned to the two boys who'd walked up beside him. "He's Noel. That's Freddie."

Both gave pounds to Diego, Speedy, and Hudson.

"That kid with the Mohawk over there is Carmelo," Kasaan said, pointing. "The kid next to him is Andre." Andre was wearing the Houston Rockets socks.

"Yo, where are you from?" Diego kicked off the wall and floated back on his noodle.

"We can't come in until Coach B. gets here." Kasaan grabbed the ends of the towel around his neck. "She'd send us home if we went in without her again."

"What's the name of your team?" Speedy asked.

"Check out that hoop!" Andre said. He started walking around the pool.

"Where you going?" Kasaan said.

"Coach B. better get here soon," Andre said, tossing his towel onto a chair and kicking off his flip-flops. "That's all I have to say."

"Andre, man," Noel said, "you have to wait."

He stopped by Red, Maya, and me and fist-bumped Red, who was sitting on the side of the pool. "I'm Andre."

"Hakeem 'the Dream' Olajuwon played for the Houston Rockets," Red said, looking at his socks. "Hakeem 'the Dream' Olajuwon of the Houston Rockets was the NBA Most Valuable Player in 1994. Hakeem 'the Dream' Olaju- won of the Houston Rockets was the Most Valuable Player of the NBA Finals in 1994 and 1995."

"Send that up." Andre motioned to the ball floating near Zoe.

"Andre, man, you have to wait," Noel said again. "C'mon."

"One shot," Andre said.

Maya passed him the ball.

"It'll be fine." He headed for the diving board. "There's no slide at this pool, so I can't get in trouble for . . ."

The door to the pool area opened. A woman walked in. She pointed at Andre.

"I know you weren't about to—"

"No way, Coach B.," Andre said, cutting her off and smacking the ball. "I was . . . I was just scoping things out."

With a tilt of the head, she told him to get rid of the ball.

He passed it down to me. Diego snatched it out of my hands.

The door to the pool area opened again. Coach Acevedo walked in.

"My crew is just getting out," he said, heading for Coach B.

"That's not necessary," she said. "My guys can wait."

"No, no, no," Coach Acevedo said. "We've been in long enough, and they need to be at dinner in twenty minutes."

"Twenty minutes?" She laughed. "Good luck with that."

"Look out below!" Diego shouted.

With the ball raised over his head, he charged off the diving board and leaped toward the hoop.

"Boom! In your . . ."

Splash!

Night Talk

"**Can a ram kill me,** Charlie 'Mega-Man' Roth?" Red asked.

"Definitely," Mega-Man answered.

"What about a deer?" Red said. "Can a deer kill me?"

"Definitely," Mega-Man said again.

Diego and I cracked up.

We were in our hotel room playing can-this-animal-kill-me. It's not really a game, but it felt like one. Red was twirling a mini-basketball in his lap on the cot at the foot of my bed. He had a cot because Red doesn't like sharing a bed. Mega-Man and Diego had the other bed. Mega-Man was sitting against the headboard. Diego was perched on the edge of the mattress. I had the other big bed all to myself. I had given up trying to spin a basketball on my finger and was just relaxing.

"Can a falcon kill me?" Diego asked.

"Definitely," Mega-Man said.

"A falcon can't kill me." He picked up a mini plastic football and started tossing it at the ceiling.

"Yes, it can," Mega-Man said.

"The peregrine falcon can dive at two hundred miles per hour. It would take you out like that." He snapped his fingers. "But peregrine falcons mostly go for ducks."

Suddenly, Diego dove onto my bed. "Odell!" he shouted as he pretended to make a diving catch.

Diego had been diving from bed to bed like that for a while. Each time, he called out the name of another wide receiver, like "Dez!" or "Megatron!" or "Amari!"

I checked the connecting door. We'd closed it about a half hour ago when Ms. Yvonne and the girls went back to their suite down the hall. When they left, Coach Acevedo had told us not to stay up much longer. At any moment, I was expecting him to pop in and tell us to keep it down or to say "Lights out."

"What about an owl?" I asked. "Can an owl kill me?"

"Some owls fly super fast," Mega-Man said. "They could dive-bomb into you like a peregrine falcon and take you out. Owl vomit looks like turd."

"Turd!" Diego dove back onto his bed.

"Turd!" Red and I said at the same time.

We all laughed. Some words make fifth graders laugh. They just do.

I stared at Mega-Man. He was finally talking. He still seemed strange, but not nearly as strange as he did on the bus and at the pool. I think he liked it better with fewer kids around.

"How do you know so much about animals?" Diego asked.

Mega-Man laughed. "*Wild Kratts*!"

"Yo, I used to love that show," Diego said.

"Me too, Diego Vasquez," Red said. "I used to watch *Wild Kratts* all the time."

"My aunt is a veterinarian," Mega-Man added. "During the summer, I work at her animal hospital. I'm working there next week over vacation."

"What do you do there, Charlie 'Mega-Man' Roth?" Red asked.

"He picks up turds!" I said, laughing.

"Steaming fresh turds!" Diego bounced to his knees.

We all laughed again.

"I do all different things." Mega-Man adjusted the pillow behind his head. "One time, I got to watch a horse give birth. This other time, there was this goat that got really sick and . . ." He stopped and looked at Diego. "Did you think you were going to die?"

The basketball rolled off my finger and onto the floor.

"What?" Diego asked.

"You're the kid with cancer, right?" Mega-Man said.

"Yeah." Diego gripped the mini football.

"I've never met anyone my age with cancer," Mega-Man said.

"Yeah, you have." Diego sat down.

I placed my palms on the bed. I'd never heard anyone ask Diego about his cancer. Not like this. I checked Red. He was pinky-thumb-tapping his leg. His eyes were glued to Diego.

"What was the worst part?" Mega-Man asked.

"Probably when I found out how bad it was. Or maybe when I first heard the word *cancer*. Or . . ." He paused. "I don't know. There were lots of worst parts."

Whenever anyone talked about Diego being sick, it always used to freak me out. Especially when they said the word *cancer*. But right now, I wasn't freaked out at all. Come to think of it, I hadn't been the other day at practice either.

I stared at Mega-Man. He was asking the questions I wanted to know the answers to but would never ask. Not in a gazillion years.

What's it like having Coach Crazy for a father? Does he act like that at home? Did that ref press charges?

Those were the questions I wanted to ask Mega-Man but never would. Not in a gazillion years.

"One of the worst parts was also one of the best parts," Diego said.

"What do you mean?" I asked.

"My uncle was one of the worst parts," Diego said softly. "What I put him through, what I put him and my moms through. Yo, my uncle was there for me the whole time. The whole time." He picked at the tip of the football. "My uncle was also one of the best parts because . . . he's a hero. A real hero. I wouldn't be here without him. My uncle is the best."

"Ducks are the best," Mega-Man blurted.

Diego and I looked at one another. "What?" we said at the same time.

"Ducks are my favorite animals," Mega-Man said.

"Where did that come from?" Diego asked.

"They are." Mega-Man pulled the buds off his neck and put them on the table between our beds. "Next week, my aunt's taking me to this pond to check out the ducks."

Diego laughed. "How do you do that?"

"Do what?" Mega-Man asked.

"One minute you're asking me if I thought I was going to die, and the next minute you're talking about duck ponds! What are you going to talk about next, oyster poop?"

"Oyster poop!" Red and I said together.

I laughed so hard I rolled off my bed. Red rolled off his cot. Yeah, Red was on the floor. Up until a few months ago, Red would never even *sit* on a floor.

"Ducks don't have thingies," Mega-Man said.

"Thingies?" I said.

"You know," Mega-Man said, pointing to his privates.

"Get out!" Diego said, popping back up. "How can they not?"

"They don't."

"Who told you that?" I asked.

"They don't," Mega-Man said. "Their thingies are like corkscrews and—"

"Ha!" I cut him off. "So they do have thingies."

"Thingy, thingy, thingies!" Diego plopped back down.

Mega-Man shook his head. "When they're about to mate, they unfurl and circle around the females."

"Stop!" Diego laughed. He rolled off the bed and landed between Red and me. "I can't take it!"

"Their thingies are really big," Mega-Man said. "They have to keep them inside their body."

Diego, Red, and I laughed harder and louder. I rolled onto Diego and kicked my feet against the side of the mattress.

Mega-Man crawled to the end of the bed and looked over at us. "Mallards are sexually dimorphic."

"Sexually dimorphic!" Diego smacked the floor with both hands.

"A lot of songbirds are," Mega-Man said.

"What does that even mean?" I asked.

"Males and females look different. Males have dark and shiny green heads with yellow bills. Females are brown with orange and brown bills. One sex—"

"Sex!" Red laughed harder than I'd ever seen him laugh. "Charlie 'Mega-Man' Roth said *sex*!"

Bumper-Vators

I gripped the doorknob. In a moment, we were leaving the hotel room and heading down to breakfast. Then it was off to the Showdown.

Then I was going to see *him*.

"Yes, yes, yes!" Diego shouted, leaping from bed to cot to bed.

Diego had been bouncing around the room from the second he got up. He woke Mega-Man and me by hitting us with a pillow. He was about to do the same to Red, but I'd stopped him just in time.

"Yes, yes, yes!" Diego bounded to Red and double-high-fived him. "It's Showdown Saturday!"

"Oh, yeah!" Red said. "It's Showdown Saturday."

It was Showdown Saturday, but my stomach felt like it did Halloween night when I ate those twenty bite-size Three Musketeers.

"Move, move, get out of the way!" Diego shoved me aside

and opened the door. "Yes, yes, yes!" He charged down the hall toward the elevator. "Breakfast!" he shouted. "All-you-can-eat bacon and sausage!"

Mega-Man and Red raced after him. I followed. When I reached the elevator, Diego was still trying to press the Down button by jump-kicking it. I shoulder-shoved him out of the way and pushed it.

A few seconds later the doors opened.

"Wait for us!" Maya called from the other end of the hall.

"You'd better hurry," Diego said to the girls coming out of their room.

I stepped onto the elevator and pressed the Door Open button. "We're holding it," I said, shoving Diego again.

He pushed me back and knocked me into the button panel. "Bumper-vators!"

"Dag," I said.

"Bumper-vators!" he repeated.

"Bumper what?"

"It's a game." Diego bobbed his head and smiled. "You'll see."

I wasn't in the mood for Diego's bumper game, whatever it was. Then again, I wasn't in much of a mood for anything.

"Good morning, gentlemen," Ms. Yvonne said as she and the girls reached the elevator.

"The ladies have arrived!" Maya said. "Let's get this party started!"

Ms. Yvonne looked at Red. "You okay on here, honey?"

Red stood against the back wall, looking up at the ceiling and pinky-thumb-tapping his leg. Red doesn't like tight quarters. The other times we rode the hotel elevator, Mega-Man, Diego, and I had been the only ones with him.

Ms. Yvonne stepped around Mega-Man and Mimi and moved next to Red.

"When I was in the hospital," Diego said as the door closed, "these kids taught me this game called bumper-vators."

Maya made a face. "Why do I already know I'm not going to like it?"

The elevator started moving.

"You pretend you're a bumper car at an amusement park," Diego said. He pushed me again, harder than last time. My cheek hit the panel, and I knocked into Mega-Man.

"Dag!" I said.

With both forearms, I shoved him back. Diego stumbled into Zoe and A-Wu, who slammed into the back wall.

"Yes, yes, yes!" Diego laughed.

"Guys, I don't think this is such a good idea," Ms. Yvonne said.

"This is bumper-vators." Diego shoulder-shoved Mega-Man into the wall and then charged me.

"No!" Ms. Yvonne shouted.

"No, no, no!" I blocked Diego's hands and grabbed one of his wrists. "No, no, no!" With my basketball eyes, I pointed to Red.

He was squatting in the corner behind Mimi and Maya. He had his arms in front of his head like a boxer covering up.

"Game over!" Ms. Yvonne said firmly. "Enough."

"No bumper-vators!" I said.

"No bumper-vators." Diego held up his arms. "Game over."

"Red, no more bumper-vators," I said.

"Honey, honey, honey," Ms. Yvonne said. She touched Red's shoulder. "It's okay." She shot Diego a look. "You need to calm down!"

"Game over," Diego said again. "Yo, my bad, Red. Game over."

Ping.

The *L* on the button panel lit.

Ms. Yvonne kneeled next to Red. "Honey, it's okay."

Red was shaking. His arms covered his face. His fists tapped his head.

The doors opened.

"You okay, Red?" I squatted in front of him and put my hand on his shoulder as most of the others got off.

"No bumper-vators," he said. "No bumper-vators, no bumper-vators."

"No bumper-vators, Red," I said. "No more bumper-vators."

"Honey, no more bumper-vators," Ms. Yvonne said. "I promise."

"No bumper-vators," Red kept saying. "No bumper-vators."

"Yo, my bad, Red," Diego said. "That was uncool of me. My bad."

"That was a very poor decision." Ms. Yvonne shook her head at Diego.

He frowned. "My bad."

"You okay, Red?" I asked again.

Slowly, he lowered his arms.

"You boys need to calm down," Ms. Yvonne said. "You can't go into breakfast out of control like this." She rubbed Red's back. "Take your time, honey."

"I'm okay," he said softly.

"It's all good, Red," I said.

"Sorry, Red," Diego said, grimacing.

"I'm okay, Diego Vasquez." Red loosened his fists. "I'm okay." He let out a long breath and dropped his shoulders.

"Take your time, honey," Ms. Yvonne said again.

Red looked from me to Diego and slowly stood. "I'm okay."

"Honey, here's what we're going to do," Ms. Yvonne said.

"You and I are going to take a little walk before we go in to breakfast. We're going to get some fresh air, okay?"

Red nodded.

"Let me go run ahead and tell Coach Acevedo," she said, stepping off the elevator. "I'll be right back."

"You'd better be," Diego said, leaping off the elevator. "It's all-you-can-eat sausage and bacon!"

I gave Red a double pound. "You good?"

"I'm good, Mason Irving."

I stepped off the elevator and stopped dead in my tracks.

Who's Your Daddy?

"Hey, pal!"

I opened my mouth to speak, but words didn't follow. I was standing face-to-face with *him*.

"Look at you!" he said, smiling proud. He stepped toward me with his arms out.

I backed away.

"Look at you," he said again. He placed his hands on his head. "You must've grown half a foot since last time I saw you."

"What are you doing here?" I said. I was trembling. He had to see that I was.

"I can't get over you," he said. "Last time I saw you, you were up to here." He held the side of his hand to his chest and reached out with the other. "Check out those dreads."

"Dag." I ducked away.

"Respect." He held up his hand. "They look great on you, pal."

"What are you doing here?" I asked again.

"Lesley told you I was coming. You knew I—"

"Here," I interrupted. "What are you doing *here*? At the hotel?"

"I figured I'd come by and introduce myself. Maybe grab some grub."

I dug my hands into my pouch pocket and hid my shaking fists.

He looked exactly as I remembered. Exactly. He was wearing jeans again, but this time he had on a zipped-up brown bomber jacket and white sneakers.

"I can't get over how tall you've gotten." He gripped the back of his neck and looked to my left. "You must be one of . . . Red? No way!"

I was so focused on my father I'd forgotten Red was beside me. His neck was turtled deep into his hoodie. Both his hands pinky-thumb-tapped his legs. I didn't know if it was because of my father, because of the elevator, or both.

"Good to see you, Red." My father held out his hand.

Red's hands didn't leave his legs. "Hi, Rip's Dad."

"He doesn't bite," Diego said.

Diego was on the other side of me. I'd forgotten he was here, too.

"And who might you be?"

"I'm Diego Vasquez." He held out his hand.

My father shook it. "David Irving. Nice to meet you, Diego Vasquez."

"Thanks for helping out Clifton United," Diego said, resting his arm on my shoulder. "We really appreciate it."

"It's the least I can do."

"Rip's a beast on the court, Mr. Irving." Diego tapped my chin with his elbow. "Wait till you see him play. Lives up to his Rip Hamilton nickname."

"Rip Hamilton nickname?" He eyed me.

"Rip Hamilton," Diego said. "Old-school Detroit Pistons player."

"Interesting."

I tightened my shaking fists and pressed my knuckles together.

"No offense, Mr. Irving," Diego said, bobbing his head, "but you weren't what I was . . . You and Rip look nothing alike."

He smiled. "We get that a lot."

"We do?" I snapped.

"We used to." He reached for my shoulder.

I dodged it.

My father was white with light hair. I'm black with dark hair.

"I can't wait to see you run ball, pal," he said, smiling proud again.

"Okay."

"I'm looking forward to spending the day with the team."

"Yeah."

He gripped the back of his neck and glanced over his shoulder. "I tell you what," he said, "I think it might be easier if I meet everyone over at Hoops Haven. Sound good?"

"Whatever."

"I'll see you over there." He held out his fist.

I left him hanging.

Breakfast of Champions

"Brrrr," **Diego said,** rubbing his arms and pretending to shiver. "That was chilly."

I placed my elbows on the table and pressed my palms to my temples.

Diego bobbed his head and smiled. "You and your dad seem really tight."

We were the only ones at our circular booth next to the area where the breakfast buffet was served. The rest of Clifton United was getting their food or sitting at the long, high table that cut across the lobby.

I was shaking. I hadn't stopped since the elevator.

"No way are you going to eat all that," Maya said, walking up and motioning to Diego's tray.

"Watch me," he said. "This is my breakfast of champions before the tournament of champions!"

Diego had three full plates of food on his tray. One had a stack of pancakes and a mound of scrambled eggs. Another had two bagels and three blueberry muffins. The third was all bacon and sausage, and at the moment, he was stuffing bacon strips into his hoodie pouch.

"Dessert for the bus ride," he said, still bobbing his head.

Even though the breakfast was all-you-can-eat, I only took an English muffin. After two bites, I already felt like I needed to puke.

Maya slid into the booth across from me. "That's all you're eating?"

"Not hungry," I said.

"He just saw his father," Diego said.

I shot him a look.

"What?" He sucked down the strip of bacon that was dangling out of his mouth like it was a strand of spaghetti.

"What's wrong with your father?" Maya asked.

"From what I was able to gather," Diego said, "they're not exactly close."

Ms. Yvonne and Red walked up. Ms. Yvonne sat down next to Maya. Red slid in next to me so that he was facing the door *and* so he could watch *SportsCenter* on the flat screen over the fireplace.

"You're not eating?" Ms. Yvonne said to me.

I shook my head.

"I don't think Rip and his dad get along," Diego said.

"Shut up, Diego."

"I'm sorry I missed him," Ms. Yvonne said. "I'm looking forward to meeting him."

"I'm looking forward to thanking him," Maya said. "We wouldn't be here without him."

"He saved our butts," Diego said.

With my basketball eyes, I checked Red. His eyes were fixed on *SportsCenter* as he ate the top of his chocolate chip muffin. Red only eats muffin tops. He twists off the bottoms and gives them to me. He put the bottom on my plate.

Diego took it. "You going to tell us what's up with your—"

"My father left when I was in first grade," I said. I spoke softly. "He took a job in Hong Kong."

Ms. Yvonne, Maya, and Diego all stared. Red's eyes stayed with the NBA playoff preview, but I could tell he was listening to everything.

"My mom and him were already thinking about separating," I said. "So he went. It was a five-year commitment."

Diego waved his fork. "That's it?"

"What do you mean?"

"I thought he did something terrible. Like he had a secret family or he and your mom got into some big—"

"He didn't want to be with us," I snapped. I gripped the back of my neck. "He chose work over his family."

"If you say so."

"Shut up, Diego."

* * *

On the bus to Hoops Haven, I sat up front again. The rest of Clifton United sat in the back. Even Mega-Man did. Diego and Red offered to sit with me, but I told them I wanted to be alone for a few minutes.

I twisted a lock above my ear at its root. We were about to walk into Hoops Haven. He was going to be there. For the rest of the day, he was going to be with Clifton United.

I had to shift into basketball mode. No matter what. I had to be all basketball.

"Bacon?" Diego slid into the seat beside me and held out a strip.

I shook my head.

"I came to see how you're doing." He popped the bacon into his mouth.

"I'm fine."

"You look it." Diego bobbed his head and chewed. Then he wiggled his fingers in front of my face. "I see a bundle of joy. Rainbows, unicorns, twinkling stars, and—"

"I'm fine." I leaned away.

"Yo, it's the Showdown, Rip." He pulled another piece of bacon from his pouch. "You can't let this ruin it. Whatever *this* is."

"You don't understand."

"Maybe not, but I do understand one thing." He shook his fingers. "This is the Showdown."

Pool Team

"Ballin'!" Maya said as Clifton United walked into the office area of Hoops Haven.

"We're ranked number two," A-Wu said, pointing to the ginormous scoreboard on the wall.

The scoreboard looked like March Madness brackets, but none of the pairings had been posted yet. All the teams were listed on the side.

I checked the office. I didn't see him.

"We're not number two," Mega-Man said, and flicked A-Wu's ear. "The teams are in alphabetical order."

The office was located above the field house courts. I could hear the bouncing balls, squeaking sneakers, and echoing voices coming from the other side of the large window behind where the tournament officials were seated.

"Hang out here for a sec," Coach Acevedo said. He thumbed the officials. "Let me find out where we need to be."

The office door opened. I flinched. Some teenagers carrying mesh bags of basketballs walked in. One of them held the door for the grown-up behind him, who was pushing a hand truck loaded with bottled water.

With both hands, I gripped the locks above my neck. Diego, Zoe, and Super-Size stood by the window looking at the courts. Maya, Red, and Mega-Man were passing around a basketball. Where was he? He had to be here. Was he down by the courts? Was he still outside? Was he—

I wobbled. He was with Coach Acevedo. Shaking hands with Coach Acevedo. Smiling proud and motioning my way.

"Is that your dad?" Maya asked. She caught the pass from Mega-Man and faced me.

"Yeah."

My stomach felt like Halloween night again. Only a gazillion times worse.

"Yo, the courts are sick!" Diego bounded over. "Come check them out."

My eyes stayed on Coach Acevedo and my father.

Diego rested his arm on my shoulder. "You okay?"

I swallowed. "I think so."

"Let's do this." Diego jump-turned to Mimi and gave her double pounds. "Let's do this."

"Let's circle up," Coach Acevedo said. He waved the

team to the corner with one hand and rested the other on my father's shoulder. "I'd like to introduce you to the person who came through big-time for Clifton United. This is . . . What do you want us to call you?"

My father shrugged. "You can call me . . . call me . . . call me David." He looked at me.

My eyes stayed on Coach Acevedo.

"Thanks, David." Maya waved.

Speedy reached out and shook his hand.

"I'm Yvonne Rivera," Ms. Yvonne said, and stepped forward. "Very nice to meet you. Thank you so much."

"Good to see you again, David," Diego said, waving his arms over his head and grinning.

"Good to see you again, too, Diego."

"Good to see you again, Rip's Dad," Red added.

"Red." My father chin-nodded. "Great seeing you here, pal."

"I have our schedule," Coach Acevedo said.

"Who do we play?" Zoe asked.

"We play a team called the Renegades first. That's on court two at eight forty-five."

"Yo, this is going to be sick!" Diego jumped in circles. "I'm fired up, fired up, fired up!"

"At eleven," Coach Acevedo said, "we're over on court six playing a team called Almond."

"Almond?" Mega-Man and Super-Size said at the same time.

"That's what they told me," Coach Acevedo said. "These pool-play games determine the seedings for the next round."

My eyes still hadn't left Coach Acevedo. I had to be all basketball. No distractions, no matter what.

Easier said than done.

The office door opened again. This time, another team walked in. It was the team from the pool. They were all wearing black hoodies and black shorts. Some had on head-phones.

"How's it going, guys?" Hudson said.

"Yo, what's up?" Diego said.

None of them answered. None of them looked our way. They just walked straight to the door with the sign TO COURTS 1–8 above it.

Coach B. nodded to Coach Acevedo as she passed. She didn't break stride.

"Whoa," I said after they'd all left.

"That was weird," Mehdi said.

"That was cold," Speedy added.

"That was gamesmanship," Coach Acevedo said. "Ordinarily, I'd say if you don't know what *gamesmanship* means, look it up when you get home. But since we're not going home for a while, I'll tell you."

"Head games," I said.

"Exactly," Coach Acevedo said. "It's a way of getting into your opponent's head. It's a little questionable at this level, but it's perfectly legal." He drew a circle in the air with his finger. "Don't let them play you. Don't be psyched out."

Renegades

By the time we got downstairs to court two, the Renegades were already warming up. The Renegades were the team from the pool *and* the team from the lobby.

We were completely psyched out.

I stepped off our pregame layup line, folded my arms, and stared. Their uniforms were fresh—black and silver reversible jerseys, black shorts, black-and-white socks, and black high-tops. They could ball, too. Seriously ball. Carmelo, the kid with the Mohawk, was going to be a monster under the boards. Another kid with a Mohawk had a deadly outside shot. So did Andre. So did Noel. So did Freddie.

I locked eyes with Kasaan, the kid from the pool who'd been all smiley and friendly. He was still all smiley, but this smile had an edge. He pinched the number five on his jersey, squared up, and took a shot from just inside the three-point circle.

Swish.

I looked away. My eyes went right to my father standing

next to Ms. Yvonne along the sideline across from our team bench.

My stomach churned. I was the floor general. I was supposed to be rising to the occasion. But right now, with Clifton United minutes from the opening tip of the Showdown—our first-ever tournament game—I was thinking about the man across the gym with the brown bomber jacket draped over his arm.

I smacked the side of my head. Hard.

I stepped back onto the rebounding line just in time to see Hudson fire a brick that didn't even hit rim. A-Wu rebounded the miss and lobbed a lollipop pass to Speedy. She drove to the hoop for her layup, but as she went up she lost the handle and the ball sailed out of bounds.

"Pick it up, United!" Diego clapped hard. "C'mon now. A little energy!"

Completely. Psyched. Out.

* * *

"Should we just go home now?" Coach Acevedo asked. We'd circled up near the foul line. "That's what it looks like we want—"

"No way," Diego interrupted angrily. His fists were clenched by his sides. "We're here to play ball."

"That's not what our body language is saying." Coach

Acevedo shook the basketball he held with both hands. "Our body language is saying we already lost."

"Let's go, Clifton United!" Red said, squinching his face. "We're here to play."

"We come committed." Diego stepped into the circle and clapped hard. "C'mon, Clifton United!"

I grabbed the back of my neck and looked across the court. I could see . . .

"C'mon, Rip!" Diego shouted.

My eyes shot back to the huddle.

Diego was pointing at me. "Yo, we need you here!" he said.

"Easy, Diego," Coach Acevedo said.

"I'm playing for Clifton United in a basketball tournament." Diego thumped his chest. "You know how much that means to me. You know—"

"Enough, Diego," Coach Acevedo said. He dropped to a knee and looked at us. "We're pushing reset." He pressed his thumb to the floor. "We just hit the reset button."

Red took a knee and smacked the floor with both hands. Then Maya did. Then Super-Size did. Then the rest of us did.

"Our Showdown starts now," Coach Acevedo said. "No hanging heads, no slumping shoulders, no defeated faces. Clifton United's Showdown starts now." He flipped the ball to Red. "You ready to rise to the occasion?"

"We will rise to the occasion, which is life, Coach Acevedo," Red said.

He pointed Red to the line. "Go make your shot."

Red hustled to the line. He trapped the ball under his foot and took several breaths. Then he picked up the ball, squared his shoulders, and sized up the rim.

For less than a nanosecond, my eyes darted to *him*.

Red dribbled three times—low and hard—and stood back up. He spun the ball until his fingers found the right seams and then looked at the rim again. He extended his arms and took the free throw.

Swish!

The Opener

Mimi, Speedy, Diego, and I lined up around the circle. Super-Size set up for the jump against Carmelo.

I checked the scoreboard on the wall beyond the baseline.

HOME 0   VISITOR 0

The Renegades were the home team.

My basketball eyes checked my father. He still stood with Ms. Yvonne and smiled proud.

"Good luck, everyone," the referee said. She stepped to the middle and raised the ball. "Players, hold your spots."

Super-Size had decent ups, but no way was he winning the tip, and I could tell Carmelo was looking to back-tap to Mohawk-2.

I was right.

Mohawk-2 caught the tip over his head, and then like a soccer player throwing an inbounds, he fired a pass up to

Andre on the right. Andre took two dribbles and put up a shot from behind the three-point line.

Swish!

"Dag," I said under my breath.

Eight seconds in, we were already down three.

"Let's go, United," Coach Acevedo said, clapping. "Run the offense, Rip."

I brought the ball up. I was getting the ball to Diego. This was his first game. This was his first possession. The ball had to go to Diego.

I passed to him on the wing. He sent the ball to Mimi in the corner. She dribbled once and passed it back. Diego stared down his man and jab-stepped a couple times, but when his man didn't go for the fake, he passed to me. I sent it right back to him.

"Take your shot!" I said.

He did.

Swish!

"Yes!" Diego leaped into the air. He high-fived me hard as he sprinted back on defense. "Let's do this!"

Our whole bench stood and cheered.

"Way to go, Diego Vasquez!" Red shouted, waving his towel. "Let's go, defense!"

The Renegades came right back and scored another quick basket. Kasaan lofted a pass over our defense to Mohawk-2 for an easy deuce.

"Run Black Widow," Coach Acevedo said to me as I brought the ball up.

I thought-bubbled the play.

"Black Widow," I called. "Black Widow."

Suddenly, Kasaan and Andre charged. I wasn't expecting the half-court trap. I picked up my dribble and pivoted right. With four waving arms blocking my sight lines and passing lanes, I tried spinning left . . .

Tweet! Tweet!

"No, no, no, thirty-two," the ref said, rolling her fists. "You're shuffling your feet. That's a travel. Black ball on the side."

"Shake it off, thirty-two!" a voice called from the far sideline.

I winced.

The Renegades called a set play, and once again they got the ball into Mohawk-2, close to the rim. He scored another easy basket.

Coach Acevedo called a time-out.

HOME 7   VISITOR 2

"We need to play smart out there," Coach Acevedo said in the huddle. "We can't turn the ball over. Let's keep those heads up."

I was trying to listen, but my eyes kept darting across the gym. They seemed to be doing so on their own.

"We can't let them sneak in behind our defense," Coach Acevedo went on. "We need to be sprinting back." He looked around the huddle. "Mega-Man, you go in for Mimi. Maya, let's have you sub in for Speedy." He snapped his fingers in front of my face. "You with me?"

"Huh?" I said.

"I said, are you with me?"

"Yeah, yeah." I shook out my hair.

"Show me that you are. Let's get Mega-Man involved right away. Work the ball into him."

I worked the ball into Mega-Man right away, but Carmelo blocked his shot and Kasaan beat me to the loose ball. Then Kasaan beat me downcourt and scored a breakaway layup.

"Let's go, Rip," Coach Acevedo said.

Once again, I brought the ball up, and Kasaan met me at half-court. This time, I faked to Diego and passed to Maya. But Kasaan didn't buy my fake. Not for a second. He stepped right into the passing lane and stole the ball. Then he fired a chest pass to Andre, who raced down the floor for another fast-break basket.

I clasped my hands behind my head.

"Ref, sub," Coach Acevedo said.

The ref signaled for him to make the switch. He sent Hudson in and me to the bench.

"Shake it off, thirty-two!" that voice shouted from across the gym.

I sat down in the empty chair next to where Red was standing and cheering.

"Nice playing, Mason Irving," he said.

"Really, Red?"

I grabbed the towel from the back of my chair, covered my head, and placed my hands over my face.

* * *

"Any suggestions?" Coach Acevedo asked at halftime. We huddled up under the scoreboard. "I'm serious. I'm out of ideas."

Things didn't go any better with me on the bench. We still couldn't get clean looks, and the few times we did manage to work the ball inside, the Renegades double- and triple-teamed. On defense, we switched to a two-three zone, but they destroyed us with hot outside shooting.

HOME 22   VISITOR 6

"We need to pick up the intensity," Diego said, his face tight like a knot. "Clifton United is better than this."

Diego played the whole first half. He was the only one who did. He played his heart out on every play at both ends of the floor.

"Ideas?" Coach Acevedo said. "Anyone?"

With my basketball eyes, I looked at my father. He was still standing with Ms. Yvonne, but he was no longer on the other side of the gym. He was behind Mimi and Mehdi across the huddle.

I grabbed the locks above my neck. He did ruin everything. He was ruining the Showdown.

"We're going to shake things up a little to start the second half," Coach Acevedo said. "We're going with a lineup we haven't tried yet." He looked around the huddle. "Speedy, Diego, Mehdi, Mega-Man, Super-Size—you're our five."

Diego clapped hard. "We can do this, United," he said. "Let's go!"

"Let's bring it in," Coach Acevedo said, finger-waving us closer. "We're up against quite a team, so whatever happens now happens. Let's just play hard and have fun. That's real Clifton United basketball." He placed his hand in the middle.

"Let's play some real Clifton United basketball. On three, United. One, two, three . . ."

"United!"

Coach Acevedo pulled me to the side.

"We need you leading, Rip," he said. "We need you focused."

I nodded.

"No distractions," he said. "You're our team general."

I nodded again and thought about my father.

* * *

We played real Clifton United basketball in the second half. We played hard and had fun. But there was no incredible turn of events or miraculous comeback. We lost by thirty.

Now, when I say *we* played real Clifton United basketball and had fun, that's not entirely accurate. Coach Acevedo never put me back in the game.

Showing Up

As soon as the game against the Renegades ended, Diego told Coach Acevedo he wanted to talk to me away from the team. So Coach Acevedo walked Diego and me to the far end of the field house and told us to be back at court six in twenty minutes.

We sat side by side against the wall. Kids from a team called Front Street Fury were shooting at the basket in front of us. One kid had on a protective face mask. Another wore uniform number double zero. A third kid danced around like he was on *America's Got Talent* whenever he didn't have the ball.

"When I first got sick," Diego started talking, "my moms was the one who told me news. Whenever there was any kind of update—good or bad—she was the one who told me. It was freaking me out because—"

"This is what you wanted to talk about?" I interrupted.

"Just listen."

"Diego, if you think you're going to cheer me up, you might as well—"

"Yo, just shut up for a sec."

I paused. "Fine."

"My moms was freaking me out because she wasn't

telling me everything, and I knew she wasn't. But I needed to know everything because that's how I deal with things." Diego glanced my way. "You learn a lot about how you deal with things when you have cancer."

"Sometimes you don't sound like a kid."

He laughed. "That's another thing that happens when you have cancer. You spend so much time talking to grown-ups about grown-up things that you end up sounding like a grown-up even when you're not talking to grown-ups."

A ball bounded toward Diego. He leaned over and swatted it back onto the court. Face Mask scooped it up and waved thanks.

"My uncle saw how much my moms was freakin' me out," Diego said. "He stepped up and took over. Yo, my uncle saved me."

"What did he do?"

Diego smiled. "He came up with the Gang of Three," he said. "He showed up at the hospital one day in a gladiator costume. He brought costumes for me and my moms, and made us put them on, stand in the middle of my room, raise our swords, and—"

"Swords?"

"Yo, these costumes were tight! They had swords and shields and everything. So he had us raise our swords and make a pact: Whenever there was any kind of news, the Gang of Three all had to be present for it."

"That's pretty cool."

Diego nodded. "When the doctors said I needed more chemo, we were all there to hear it. When I was running a fever, and my counts were low, and the doctor told us about the lockdown and how—"

"Lockdown?"

"It only happened one time. I couldn't leave my room or have any visitors. It was during flu season." Diego leaned forward and retied his sneaker. "Whenever there was news, I got to see their faces. That's what I needed. My uncle did that. My uncle's the best."

"That's what you said last night."

"He is. Before I got sick, the only other kid I ever knew with cancer was this kid Silas, one of my uncle's co-worker's kids. But he died. So when I found out I had cancer, I thought I was going to die."

"Not everyone dies from cancer," I said.

"Ooh!" Diego pointed in my face. "You said the *c-word*!"

"So?"

"You've never said it before."

"Yeah, I have."

But I hadn't. Not in front of Diego. Not even last night in the hotel room.

"It's fine you don't like saying it," Diego said. "I know other people who don't."

"Not everyone dies from it."

"Duh." He bumped my shoulder. "I'm here."

"I'm glad."

"Me too."

I bumped him back. "Cancer, cancer, cancer."

He laughed. "That's better."

Another ball bounced our way. I caught it with both hands and threw it back to Dancing Man.

"Your father seems pretty cool, Rip," Diego said. "He reminds me of my uncle."

I pulled up my legs and wrapped my arms around my knees.

"What's the deal with you and him?"

"Nothing," I said.

"C'mon." He bobbed his head. "I told you stuff. Now you tell me."

"No."

"You know you want to." He poked my side. "C'mon."

I tried not to smile. "Remember *The Wizard of Oz*?" I asked.

"I wasn't there for it. That was right after I got sick."

"Oh, my bad."

"No, it's fine. What about it?"

"That was the last time I saw my father."

"Yo, that's a long time ago."

"I know."

"You said he left in first grade."

I nodded. "I hated it when he came back to visit. We always ended up having these huge family fights. I never wanted to see him. *The Wizard of Oz* was the last time."

Another ball headed toward us. Diego sprang to his feet and scrambled after it. He scooped it up with one hand and flipped it to Double Zero.

"Your father's back for good now?" Diego said.

"He'll be back before the end of the year," I said. "He's here this week looking for a place to live."

"Your moms says he's not a bad guy."

I unwrapped my arms from my knees and crossed my legs.

"Yo, you should listen to her," Diego said. "Your moms knows things."

I smiled. "It's a little scary sometimes."

"More than any mom I know! She helped me and my family so much. Remember that meeting with all the parents?" He poked my side again. "Cootie Man, Cootie Man!"

I bobbed my head like him. "My moms is the best."

"Nice."

"Life is about playing the cards you're dealt," I said. "That's what she always tells me, but when it comes to my father, he—"

"He wants to be present, Rip," Diego said, cutting me off. "Your dad wants to be present. Do you have any idea how many kids would give anything to have that?"

I let out a puff. "I know, but . . . he can't leave again." I gripped the back of my neck. "I hated it when he came to visit because . . . because I knew he was never staying. He was always leaving." I looked at Diego. "I couldn't stand to see him leave. It killed me. Each time, it killed me." I let out another puff. "He can't leave again."

Diego rested his arm on my shoulder. "He's not going anywhere."

"You don't know that."

"Actually, I do." He bobbed his head and smiled still again. "Yo, that's another thing you learn when you have cancer. You learn people—who's showing up and who's not. Trust me, your father wants to be here. He's not going anywhere."

"Do you know . . . Do you ever see your father?" I asked.

"He only liked being around for the good parts. Not the other stuff. The way I see it, my uncle is my real dad." He lifted his arm off my shoulder. "Yo, sorry for all the 'who's your daddy' stuff."

"What do you mean?"

"I say that to you all the time."

"I say it, too."

"I'm not going to anymore. It's not cool." He held out his fist.

I tapped it with the back of my knuckles.

"You know what I wish?" Diego said. "I wish I had a best friend like you do."

"What are you talking about?"

"I wish I had a best friend. Like you and Red."

"You're friends with everyone, Diego."

"Friendly," he said, "not friends. There's a big difference. What you and Red have . . . Speak of the devil." He pointed across the floor.

Red and Ms. Yvonne were on the other side of the court.

"There you are!" Red shouted. He charged our way.

Ms. Yvonne waved and headed off.

"Hi, Mason Irving. Hi, Diego Vasquez." He grabbed a chair from the scorer's table and dragged it over. "What are you doing?"

Diego gave him a double pound. "We're talking about toenail clippers."

"Huh?" I said.

Red sat down. "Why are you talking about toenail clippers?"

"My uncle has ten pairs of toenail clippers," Diego said, grinning. "One for each toe."

"No way," I said.

"Why does your uncle have one pair of toenail clippers for each toe?" Red asked.

"No idea," Diego answered. "I know all of my relatives' weird habits. Even the weird habits I don't want to know."

"Is that another thing you learn when you have cancer?" I asked.

"You know it!"

"Have you decided if you're coming to the Showdown, Mason Irving?" Red asked.

I made a face. "What do you mean?"

"Have you decided if you're coming to the Showdown?"

"I'm right here."

"But you haven't been here, Mason Irving, and Clifton United needs you here. Clifton United needs you to show up."

Diego stomped his feet. "Yo, I couldn't have timed that any better if I tried." He double-high-fived Red and then put his arm back on my shoulder. "That's exactly what I've been trying to tell you."

"I came to the Showdown," Red said. "You have to be here, too."

"Thanks, Red," I said.

"Thanks for what, Mason Irving?"

"For everything."

"See?" Diego pointed at Red and me. "This is what I wish I had."

"You do," I said. "We're like the Gang of Three."

"The Gang of Three!" Red said. "I like that, Mason Irving. I like that, Diego Vazquez. The Gang of Three."

Differently Dazzling

By the time we got to court six, the rest of Clifton United was already in layup lines. When Ms. Yvonne saw me, she told me to go up to the office. That's where Coach Acevedo was.

"Over here, Rip," he said when I came off the stairs.

"Hey, Coach." I stepped around the grown-ups by the officials' table and the kids checking the scoreboard. "Ms. Yvonne told me to come up."

"You doing better?" he asked.

"Much," I said.

"I thought talking to Diego would help. Our little friend can be quite spirited from time to time, but when it comes to certain matters, he's wise about things I hope I never have to be."

We moved farther away from the scoreboard and stood by the window overlooking the courts.

"So here's the deal," he said. "We're about to get our you-know-whats handed to us again down there."

"What kind of attitude is that?" I asked.

"A realistic one." He chuckled. "This Almond team we're playing—they're the defending champs. A couple weeks ago, they beat the Renegades by fifteen."

"Dag."

"Yeah, dag. And that was without their starting point guard."

I tapped my chest with my fist. "I guess I'll have to do something about it."

"I can't play you."

"What? Why?"

"I can't have you out there, Rip."

"Why not?"

"Not after last game." He tapped the glass. "You're not sharp right now."

"Yes, I am." I pressed my palms to my temples. I could feel myself starting to cry. "Coach, I'm telling you—"

"Stop!" he said sternly. "You're not sharp right now, and at this moment you're demonstrating that. You're not ready to be out there. Clifton United needs you to be ready."

I folded my arms across my chest and let out a hard puff.

"When we get to the knockout round," Coach Acevedo said, "teams are going to be looking past us." He pointed at the scoreboard. "They're going to take one look at that and think they're already in the next round." He placed his hand on my shoulder. "Clifton United is going to need its floor general to correct their thinking."

"Small ball," I said. "We'll beat them with small ball."

"That's exactly what we're counting on." He tapped my chest. "But first, during this game against Almond, you need to demonstrate that you're ready. I want you to dazzle me. Dazzle me differently."

"Who's looking to be dazzled?"

We turned. My dad walked up.

"Hey there, pal."

I half waved.

"I'm looking forward to seeing you play," he said. "I know—"

"I'm not playing," I said softly.

"Well, not this game," he said, "but you are the next one."

"First, I need to show my coach that I'm ready."

"I'm sure you'll do what needs to be done."

"I have to dazzle him," I said, shaking out my hair. "Dazzle him differently."

"Then that's what you'll do, pal." My father held out his fist.

I gave him a pound.

Almond

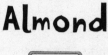

I had a great time at the game against Almond. Seriously, I did. Don't get me wrong, I would have much rather been out there playing, and I didn't exactly enjoy watching my teammates get their butts kicked and lose by thirty-three, but I had an awesome time.

It was cool cheering for the girls. In the second half, Coach Acevedo put all five in together and had them run a four-corner offense. That's a kill-the-clock strategy where the offense basically plays keep-away. We never went over the four-corner offense in practice, but the girls still nailed it. Nailed it!

It was cool cheering for Mega-Man. Yesterday at this time, we didn't even know he was on the team, and when we did find out he was, we weren't exactly thrilled. But now there he was, out there playing hard, having fun, and getting picked apart just like everyone else.

A few times during the game, I made eye contact with

my dad. He was standing with Ms. Yvonne again. Watching Clifton United play. Watching me differently dazzle. It was okay that he was here.

It was amazing cheering for Diego. Despite the whupping, he smiled the whole game.

The best was cheering next to Red. Red cheers his heart out for everyone on every play. Keeping up with him isn't exactly the easiest thing in the world, but I did.

Seedings

"I've got some good news," Coach Acevedo said, walking over. Clifton United had waited at the courts while he'd gone up to the office to find out the knockout round pairings for Saturday afternoon. "We're not the sixteenth seed."

"How's that possible?" Maya asked while tossing a ball into the air.

"One of the teams left," Coach Acevedo said. "We're actually going to be the thirteenth seed."

"How's *that* possible?" Maya asked.

"Believe it or not, another team finished behind us," Coach Acevedo said, "and according to Showdown rules, teams can't play teams they faced during pool play in the opening knockout round."

"Who do we play?" A-Wu and Mehdi asked at the same time.

"Front Street Fury."

"Yes!" I hammer-fisted the air.

That was the team shooting around when Diego and I were talking. I knew all about some of their players' games. Diego looked my way. He knew, too.

"The number-one seed is getting a bye to the second round," Coach Acevedo went on. "Since we already played the Renegades and Almond—and they're seeded two and three respectively—we're bumped to thirteen and play the number four seed. Loser goes home, winner plays the winner of the Renegades versus Strike Force."

"We're going to annihilate whoever we face!" Diego put up his fists like a boxer and shuffled his feet. "We're going to shock the world!"

"This is it!" I snatched the ball from Maya and stepped forward. "I'm here to play above and beyond Clifton United basketball."

"Real Clifton United basketball!" Mega-Man said.

"Exactly." I smacked the ball. "We're here to play real Clifton United basketball."

"It's our turn now!" Maya said. She spun to Red and gave him a loud two-handed high five.

"Oh, yeah, Maya Wade!" Red basketball-smiled. "It's our turn."

"Anything can happen." I faced Red. "Just ask Valparaiso University, right?"

"Just ask the Valparaiso University Crusaders," Red said, hopping. "Anything can happen."

"Anything *will* happen." I looked around and made eye contact with everyone. "One more *real* rise to the occasion."

Red put his hand in first. Everyone added theirs.

"We will rise to the occasion, which is life!"

Front Street Fury

At the free-throw line, Red trapped the ball under his left foot soccer-style and took a couple breaths. Then he picked up the ball, squared his shoulders, and looked at the front rim.

Along the sideline, Clifton United stood in a row, elbows locked. Coach Acevedo was at one end, Ms. Yvonne at the other.

With my basketball eyes, I checked the Fury bench. Double Zero, Face Mask, and a couple others were watching. Dancing Man and Fur—a kid with the letter *y* missing from the word *Fury* on his uniform—were examining the game ball.

Red dribbled three times—low and hard—and stood back up. He spun the ball until his fingers found the right seams and looked at the rim again. He extended his arms and took the shot.

Underhanded.

And just like every other time . . .
Swish!

* * *

"Clifton United sure looks loose out there," I play-by-played. I rubbed A-Wu's hair. "Check out what's going on at center court." Speedy rubbed my hair and Diego's at the same time. "Quite a different scene from this morning's contests, that's for sure."

We were goofing around before the opening tip, and as the Fury players took the court, they had no idea what to make of us.

Cool.

With my basketball eyes, I found my dad across the gym, kneeling down, chin in hand.

His eyes were glued to me.

I was the only kid on Clifton United with a parent here.

Cool.

Our starting five was our small-ball unit: Diego, Maya, Speedy, A-Wu, and me. A-Wu was jumping center, but we knew she wasn't outjumping Face Mask.

We had a plan.

"Here we go!" I announced. "The knockout round of the Jack Twyman Spring Showdown is under way."

Face Mask leaped for the ball, but A-Wu didn't. Instead, she backed into the circle toward where Face Mask was aiming. He tipped it too hard. The ball deflected off Fur's fingertips and out of bounds.

Plan. Executed. Perfectly.

Tweet! Tweet!

"Blue ball on the side." The referee pointed.

"Thor!" I sprinted to the spot. "Thor!"

This was the play Maya had suggested. Maya was getting the ball.

We charged into position. The Fury wasn't ready to defend a rapid-fire set play. Not even close.

I smacked the ball, and our offense went to work. A moment later, Diego was wide open up top, and Maya was wide open in the corner. I passed to her. She caught the ball, squared up, and took the shot.

Swish!

HOME 0   VISITOR 2

"Ballin'!" I pumped my fists at Maya as we sprinted back on defense.

"Ballin'!" Red stood on a chair and waved his hoodie.

Eighty-Eight, the Fury's point guard, brought the ball up, but no one was open. Our defense was on lockdown.

Maya forced Eighty-Eight into taking an off-balance shot from the foul line. It banged off the side of the backboard.

Diego boxed out Fur, grabbed the rebound, and hit me with the outlet.

"Here comes Irving," I announced. "He's got a head of steam down the left side. He crosses the three-point line . . . cuts toward lane . . . It's good! Oh, what a shot by Irving!"

"Yo!" Diego gave me a hard double pound. "Cheat code!"

I sprinted back on defense and tracked my man.

"No letdown on defense!" I shouted to my teammates. "Pick up your men!"

"Person!" Maya shouted back. "Pick up your *person*!"

I knew the Fury weren't fazed. Not at all. This was a stacked team that wasn't going away quietly. They patiently executed their half-court offense and scored on a bank shot from the elbow.

"Press! Press!" the Fury's coach shouted.

We broke their full-court press. At half-court, I dribbled past Dancing Man and made like I was heading for the lane. But just before I reached the foul line, I dumped the ball off to Diego. He faked out Fur and drove to the hoop for the basket.

"En fuego!" Diego pinched out his jersey as he raced back.

Everyone on our bench waved their hoodies.

"Diego Vasquez is unstoppable!" Red shouted. "U-N-S-T-O-P-P-A-B-L-E. Diego Vasquez is unstoppable!"

The Fury came back down the floor and worked the ball into Face Mask, who drew a foul in the act of shooting and sank one of two from the line.

The Fury didn't press after the free throws. We ran our half-court offense, but for the first time we missed a shot. The Fury grabbed the rebound and scored again.

No, they weren't going away.

HOME 5   VISITOR 6

* * *

"That was beautiful basketball out there." Coach Acevedo beamed during the first time-out. "Absolutely beautiful."

"Absolutely beautiful, Clifton United," Red said, hopping.

Everyone laughed.

"We're loose and having fun," Coach Acevedo said. "This is real Clifton United basketball."

"Above and beyond Clifton United basketball." I smacked a chair.

Coach Acevedo pointed with his iPad down the sideline. "Right now, they're making adjustments," he said. "We need to be ready."

"We're ready!" Diego pounded the floor with both fists. "Yo, we can do this!"

"We're bringing it on every possession," Coach Acevedo said. "We come committed to excellence."

Red reached over and ruffled my hair. "The Showdown is sick, Mason Irving."

"The sickest ever," I said.

* * *

The first half was twenty minutes of beautiful back-and-forth basketball. Our early four-point lead turned out to be the biggest lead for either team. A couple times, the Fury looked ready to go on a run, but each time, Maya wouldn't allow it. She made big shot after big shot and scored our last six points of the half.

Maya opened the scoring in the second half, and for the first time all game we built a five-point lead. But then Eighty-Eight took over the game. He hit two three-pointers and then made a ridiculous underhanded layup (and got fouled on the play). With four minutes left, he hit a shot from in close that gave the Fury their first lead of the half. Then a few possessions later, he and Face Mask ran a picture-perfect give-and-go.

The Fury led by four, their largest lead of the game.

HOME 38   VISITOR 34

Just 1:54 remained. We needed a basket. We were getting a basket.

We got a basket. We ran a set play, swung the ball to Super-Size near the foul line, and he hit Maya underneath for a layup.

"U-ni-ted!" our bench cheered as we raced back on defense. "U-ni-ted!"

HOME 38   VISITOR 36

The Fury ran their half-court offense and worked the ball into Face Mask. But Super-Size kept a hand in his face the whole time, so Face Mask had to swing it back out to Eighty-Eight, who put up a three-pointer.

Swish!

HOME 41   VISITOR 36

I brought the ball up. Dancing Man was still guarding me, but he was playing back.

Bad idea.

From behind the three-point line at the top of the key, I put up a shot . . .

"Boo-yah!" I hammer-fisted the air.

"Bam!" Red leaped off his chair. "Bam! Bam! Bam!"

HOME 41   VISITOR 39

"Dee-fense!" Mehdi chanted from the bench.

"Dee-fense." Everyone joined in. "Dee-fense!"

No way was the Fury scoring. No way.

Double Zero passed to Face Mask in the low post. Super-Size and I swarmed and forced him to take a bad shot.

With 41.7 seconds left, we had the ball. I walked the ball upcourt and waited for my offense. Super-Size set a screen for Maya, and as she made her cut I saw that she was going to beat her defender to the corner. My pass was waiting for her.

She took the shot.

Swish!

Tie game!

HOME 41   VISITOR 41

The Fury called their final time-out. They were going to work the clock and play for the last shot. Face Mask was going to be their first option. Dancing Man was going to be their second.

I was sure of it.

I was ready. We all were ready. We were getting the stop.

No.

Somehow, Eighty-Eight managed to thread the needle between A-Wu and Diego and get the ball to Face Mask. He put up a shot that rattled home.

"Time-out!" Coach Acevedo shouted, jabbing his fingers into his palm and forming a *T*. "Time-out!"

Tweet! Tweet!

"Time-out, blue," the referee said, and signaled.

Only 3.8 seconds remained.

`HOME 43`   `VISITOR 41`

Pacer

"An incredible game deserves an incredible finish," Coach Acevedo said in the huddle. He handed his iPad to Red. "We need our close-out play. It's time for Pacer."

"Oh, yeah!" Red smiled an above-and-beyond basket-ball smile. "I'm the man, Coach Acevedo."

"You are the man, Red."

"Who's playing where, Coach Acevedo?" he asked.

"That's your call. We're going with the same five."

Red looked at me.

I pointed to Maya. "She takes the shot," I said. "She hasn't missed all game."

"That's not completely true," Maya said, smiling. "I've missed three shots this—"

I cut her off. "You're not missing this one."

"No way," she said. "There's no way I'm missing this one."

"Maya Wade's not missing this one," Red said.

Then he went over the play.

"Mason Irving makes the pass. Eduardo 'Super-Size' Lopez and Amy 'A-Wu' Wu clear space in the middle of the court. Diego Vasquez catches the pass. Maya Wade takes the shot."

"Maya Wade *makes* the shot," she said.

"Works for me." Coach Acevedo laughed. "Hands in." He looked around the tight huddle and made eye contact with everyone. "Let's go win this game. On three, Pacer. One, two, three . . ."

"Pacer!"

* * *

"Here we go," the referee said, holding the ball out to me. "Ball's in."

Tweet! Tweet!

I jab-stepped left and broke right. Since we were taking

the ball out after a basket, I was allowed to run with the baseline, but their big man defending the inbounds didn't know that. With a clean look downcourt, I pump-faked like a quarterback and let fly. As my pass soared over the court, Super-Size and Speedy cleared room for Diego at the far key. Diego leaped for the ball and, before landing, two-handed it to Maya streaking down the sideline . . .

. . . but his touch-pass was behind her. Still, Maya somehow managed to get her fingers on the ball and tap it forward. She dribbled once with her left, picked up the ball, and then in one motion and on the run, took the shot from beyond the three-point arc.

The ball seemed to travel in slow motion . . .

Swish!

Clifton United celebrated at center court like we'd just won the Larry O'Brien Trophy.

See You Later

With my hood up and head down, I zombie-walked to the bus. Just like the rest of Clifton United.

After our win-for-the-ages against Front Street Fury, we took the court for our next game thinking the Jack Twyman Spring Showdown was *our* tournament. It didn't matter that we were facing the Renegades, the team that destroyed us by thirty in the opener. Clifton United was now a team of destiny.

Maybe not.

That thirty-point blowout looked like a nail-biter compared to what the Renegades did to us in the rematch. The Renegades scored the first nineteen points of the game. Nineteen! When you look up at the scoreboard and see your team losing 19–0, it makes you want to—

"Hey, pal!"

I turned. My father was jogging over.

"I'm glad I caught you," he said.

"We got destroyed."

"That's one way of putting it," he said. "But don't let that be your only takeaway from this weekend. It's certainly not mine."

I flipped down my hood and shook out my dreads.

"A lot of wonderful happened this weekend, Rip," he said. "Once you give yourself a moment to process everything, I think you'll see that."

"Maybe." I shrugged.

He placed a hand on my shoulder. "Let me give you another takeaway," he said. "Your nickname."

"Yeah, why did you say that back at the elevator?" I asked.

"Your nickname didn't come from Rip Hamilton of the Pistons."

"What do you mean?"

He smiled. "When you were little, you used to rip your diapers off all the time and walk around butt-naked. So your mom and I started calling you Rip."

"No way."

"Ask her." He squeezed my shoulder. "And just so you know, there's a nice surprise waiting for you back home."

"What is it?"

"You'll see when you get there. It's from the both of us."

"You're not going to tell me?"

"It's been in the works for a while now. I'm looking

forward to watching you with it when I'm back for good in the fall."

I let out a puff. "I'm glad you came this weekend."

"I am, too, Rip." He patted the side of the United Express. "Go join your teammates. I'll see you later, pal."

"Not if I see you first," I said, waving and smiling.

My dad smiled back.

When he still lived with us, on his way out of my room after he tucked me in, he would always say, "See you later." Then I would always say, "Not if I see you first." It was our thing.

Maybe one day it would be our thing again.

* * *

I sat in the back with the rest of Clifton United. Red had the window seat next to me. Diego and Speedy sat across the aisle. But on this bus ride, there was no talk of cannonball contests, chicken fights, or peeing in the bathroom. There was very little talk at all.

We didn't want to go out like this. Not after the way we beat Front Street Fury. We really thought we were going to win the rematch with the Renegades, not lose 48–11. There's nothing fun about losing 48–11.

Don't let that be your only takeaway from this weekend.

The Renegades didn't just destroy us. They humiliated us. They weren't even trying to run up the score.

A lot of wonderful happened this weekend.

I popped out of my seat and leaped over Red into the aisle. "How are your ankles?" I said to Diego.

"What?"

I stood over him. "Your ankles?" I said, smiling. "The ones that kid Kasaan broke blowing by you."

"Ooh!" a couple kids said.

"First, he broke them on that inbounds play," I said. "Then he broke them before the half. He left you sitting on your butt at the top of the key."

"He's right," Mega-Man said, grinning. "That kid absolutely—"

"What are you smiling about?" I leaped onto my seat and pointed down at Mega-Man in the row behind me. "Remember what that kid Freddie did to you?"

"I do, Mason Irving," Red said.

"Me too," Maya said, stepping to Mega-Man.

"We all do." I pretended to block a shot. "You got posterized!"

"Posterized!" Maya added.

"They schooled you, too," Mega-Man said to me.

"Don't I know it. That kid Andre stripped me clean in the backcourt, Carmelo stole two of my passes, and—"

"Carmelo stole four of your passes, Mason Irving," Red interrupted.

"Why are you counting?" I held up my hands. "Whose friend are you?"

"Everyone's!" Red basketball-smiled. "I'm everyone's friend."

Before we knew it, we were all talking and laughing and having fun again. Just like we should be. Yeah, we were bummed about the way we lost, but there was nothing we could do about it now. A lot of wonderful happened this weekend. There were a lot of takeaways.

* * *

By the time we got back to RJE, it was almost dark. Some of the kids ended up falling asleep, but most of us talked and joked the rest of the way.

As we pulled into the front circle, I looked out the window and spotted Mom and Suzanne. They were standing by Suzanne's SUV with a few other parents. I recognized most of them, but I was surprised to see one of them: Mega-Man's father, Coach Crazy.

"What are you looking at, Mason Irving?" Red asked as the bus slowed to a stop.

I pointed but didn't answer.

"Is that who I think that is?" he asked.

I nodded.

As Clifton United made their way off the bus, I knocked knuckles with my teammates as they passed. When it was Mega-Man's turn, I held out my fists.

"Nice playing with you," I said.

"You too, Rip." He topped both of them. "See you later."

I nodded once and smiled. "Not if I see you first."

I turned back toward the window and watched as my teammates reunited with their families. A-Wu ran up to her parents. She kissed her mom first and then her father. Diego greeted his uncle with a high five and a hug. Speedy gave her mom a hug, too. Her mom kissed Speedy on the top of her head.

Then it was Mega-Man's turn. He raced over to his father, dropped his bag before he reached him, and gave him a big hug. When they let go, his father ruffled Mega-Man's hair. At this moment, his father looked nothing like Coach Crazy, nothing like the Coach Crazy I knew.

Nothing like the Coach Crazy I thought I knew.

Two Days Later

"You're really not going to tell me where we're going?"
I asked.

"You'll see," Mom said, smiling.

It was the same I-know-something-good-but-I'm-not-telling-you-what-it-is smile she'd had on her face when I got back from the Showdown Saturday night. And it was the same one as yesterday's, when she kept telling me about a big surprise that would have to wait another day because the place with the big surprise was closed on Easter.

Right now, we were in the car on the way to the place with the big surprise.

"This better be worth it," I said.

"Don't worry. It will be."

I tugged on the strings of my hoodie. "I can't believe you made me get up early on the first day of spring vacation."

To be perfectly honest, I really didn't mind. I'm not a late sleeper, but that didn't mean I wanted to go anywhere. The first morning of vacation is supposed to be spent sitting on the couch in your boxers watching cartoons and playing Xbox.

"Are we going to Perky's?" I asked.

Mom claw-lifted her thermos from the console. She'd already been to Perky's. When she came in to wake me an hour ago, she said that she was running out to get coffee and that I needed to be ready by the time she got back.

"Are we meeting Dana?"

"Nope."

"Red and Suzanne?"

Mom strummed the steering wheel and shook her head.

"I'm thinking about cutting my hair," I said.

"Okay." She peeked at me. "Why's that?"

"I don't know. I think it's time."

"Cutting it all off?" she asked.

"I think so." I ran my hand over my head. "Diego said when his hair grew back, it grew in darker."

"Honey, I don't think it's possible for your hair to get much darker."

"Did you know he's had hair all year?" I lifted my legs so that my shins pressed against the glove box. "The only reason he wore a hat was because he liked being the only kid in school who was allowed to."

"That sounds very Diego."

"How much farther?" I asked.

We were driving on streets we always ride on, but I still didn't have a clue where we were going.

"Maybe two minutes," she said.

"Can I get a hint?"

"Your father knows about it and approves."

"That's not a hint." I drummed my knees. "Do you realize how annoying you're being?"

She smiled her I-know-something smile again. "Let's see if you're still saying that a few minutes from now."

"I'd better not be."

Since we got back from the Showdown, Mom had been acting very cool. Obviously, the fact that things went well between my dad and me had a lot to do with it. She wanted me to talk about it—she was dying to talk about it—but I told her I wasn't ready yet. She said we would need to at some point over vacation. That was fair.

"Okay, honey." She touched my leg. "Here's a hint: This has been in the works for a while now. Your father and I are happy and relieved you finally green-lighted it."

"I green-lighted it?"

"You really are growing up, Rip."

"Okay," I said, eyeing her sideways. "I think."

We made a left onto a road we don't often take.

"Any idea yet?" she asked.

"No."

"It's going to keep you busy."

"Is that another hint?"

"That's a big hint."

"Whatever you—" I stopped midsentence. "Don't play, Mom!" I pointed to the sign up ahead. "Is that where we're going?"

"Going where?" She smiled an extra-wide version of that smile.

"I'm getting a dog?" I said, my voice squeaking. "I can get a dog?"

We turned into the driveway of the Sean Casey Animal Rescue shelter.

"Yes, Rip," she said. "You're ready for a dog. We're getting a dog."

"Yes, yes, yes!" I shook my fists in front of my face. "We're getting a dog! We're getting a dog!"

Mom pulled into a spot and put the car in Park.

"I love you, Mom." I reached over and hugged her. "I love you, I love you, I love you!" I planted a kiss on her cheek.

She laughed. "Is this an okay surprise?"

"Okay? This is the best surprise in the history of ever!"

She held my wrist. "You will call your father to say thank you."

"Okay."

"Promise me you'll call—"

"I promise, I promise, I promise," I said. "I promise I'll call my dad and tell him thank you." I pounded the dashboard. "I'm getting Bubba!"

"Is that what you're naming it?"

"I'm getting Bubba." I kissed her cheek again. "I'm getting Bubba Chuck." I opened the door, burst from the car, and hammer-fisted the air.

"BOO-YAH!"

Acknowledgments

Thanks, respect, and love to...

Wes Adams, my editor extraordinaire. This has been and continues to be my dream project. Andrew Arnold, the designer of the series. Keep on dazzling, man. I like to be dazzled. Tim Probert, the illustrator whose drawings have added a whole other dimension to the world of Rip and Red.

Mary Van Akin, Katie Halata, Janet Renard, Joy Peskin, Lucy Del Priore, and the entire rockstar crew at Farrar Straus Giroux and the Macmillan Children's Publishing Group. Your unwavering support is humbling and heartening.

Erin Murphy, my agent. The best in the business. Yeah, I'm biased, but I speak the truth.

Elizabeth Acevedo, Anna Rekate, and Audrey Vernick, my always reliable beta readers. Your critical and caring eyes and pull-no-punches feedback are appreciated more than you can possibly imagine.

Kayley Cook, R.N., Dr. Faith Galderisi, Dr. Lori Gluck, and Dr. Craig Hurwitz, my acute myeloid leukemia experts. While most of the AML storyline ended up in the deleted darlings folder, your insights and anecdotes were invaluable.

Shana Corey and Yvonne Salgado, who provided me with the oh-so-needed mom's-eye-view of what it's like living with almost-middle schoolers.

Chris Davis, my former student, for his basketball coaching expertise. You got game.

Brenda Bowen and Virginia Euwer Wolff. We will rise to the occasion, which is life.

Kevin, my husband, my family.

GO FISH

PHIL BILDNER

What did you want to be when you grew up?
I wanted to be a basketball player or baseball player, but size and ability got in the way. I guess I wanted to be a lawyer because that's what the people in my life told me I wanted to be. Fortunately, I realized I had to be what / wanted to be.

When did you realize you wanted to be a writer?
I always loved to write, but I never considered it for a career until I was teaching middle school in the New York City public schools. My students and experiences there inspired me to write.

What's your favorite childhood memory?
Going to ball games! I loved going to Shea Stadium to watch the New York Mets, Nassau Coliseum to watch the New York Islanders, and Madison Square Garden to watch the New York Knicks.

As a young person, who did you look up to most?
I don't know if there was one person in particular that I looked up to. Of course, I had favorite athletes, musicians, and statesmen, but I don't think there was any one individual or hero that I aspired to be like more than anyone else.

What was your favorite thing about school?
In fifth grade, my teacher was Mr. Kramer. He was my first male teacher, and he ran his classroom in an unconventional manner. More than any other teacher, he made school and learning fun.

What were your hobbies as a kid? What are your hobbies now?
As a kid, I loved playing ball and playing with my dogs. I would also spend hours on my bedroom floor playing Strat-O-Matic Baseball, the precursor to fantasy baseball. My hobbies now include reading, hiking, working out, and traveling. I still love playing ball and playing with my dog (obviously, it's a different dog).

Did you play sports as a kid?
I did! I played baseball, basketball, and soccer. I always wanted to be outside running around. No matter where I went, I always looked for a pickup game of hoops.

What was your first job, and what was your "worst" job?
My first job was shoveling snow. My friend Steven and I would go around and knock on doors every time it snowed. Easy money and all cash! My worst job was when I worked at Wendy's with my friend Mitchell. We lasted two nights. Then we got a job packing bicycles and bicycle parts in a warehouse . . . which really wasn't all that much better.

What book is on your nightstand right now?
It's almost always a middle grade novel, a young adult novel, or a work of nonfiction. I'm a big fan of the Nerdy Book Club, and I try to read titles recommended on their blog.

How did you celebrate publishing your first book?

My first book was *Shoeless Joe & Black Betsy*. We had a publication party at Books of Wonder, a bookstore in New York City. At the time, I was still teaching middle school. Many of my students and their families attended. It was pretty special.

Where do you write your books?

All different places! I take a writer's notebook with me wherever I go. When I lived in the city, I would write on the subway all the time. I also enjoyed writing on the roof of my apartment building. Nowadays, most of my writing takes place either in my office at home or on my back porch. When I'm on the road, you'll find me writing on airplanes and in my hotel room. I guess I can write pretty much anywhere!

What sparked your imagination for the Rip and Red series?

When I visit schools, I always tell kids to write about what you know and love. I taught middle school for many years. I played basketball for many years. Nowadays, I visit schools around the world and interact with kids and educators in ways I never imagined. My life experiences—past and current—inspired me to write this series.

What challenges do you face in the writing process and how do you overcome them?

I don't have enough time to write all the things I want to write. The author Jeff Zentner once said to me, "I have to aggressively find the time to be creative," and as soon as he did, a lightbulb went on. I make a concerted effort to find the time to be creative every single day.

What is your favorite word?

Empathy.

SQUARE FISH

If you could live in any fictional world, what would it be?
The Hogwarts School of Witchcraft and Wizardry. Because it is the Hogwarts School of Witchcraft and Wizardry.

Who is your favorite fictional character?
Ignatius Reilly from John Kennedy Toole's *A Confederacy of Dunces*.

What was your favorite book when you were a kid? Do you have a favorite book now?
As a kid, I read the newspaper every morning. I would sit in the middle of the kitchen floor and devour the sports pages of the *New York Times*. I also read lots of sports biographies. Then in sixth grade, I read a book I wasn't allowed to read because it was supposedly too grown up for me. I read *Alive* by Piers Paul Read, the story of the rugby team whose plane crashed in the Andes Mountains. It was intense! My favorite book now? That's easy. All the ones I read aloud to my students are my all-time faves. Those were the best reading moments of my life.

If you could travel in time, where would you go and what would you do?
I would travel back in time and visit my teenage self and tell him to have the courage and conviction to be the person he really is.

What's the best advice you have ever received about writing?
Read. In order to write, you have to read. It doesn't matter what you're reading, so long as you're reading something.

What advice do you wish someone had given you when you were younger?
Live your life, not the life others want you to live or the life you think you're supposed to live.

Do you ever get writer's block? What do you do to get back on track?

I used to believe in writer's block, but I don't anymore. Philip C. Stead is right. Ideas are all around. Whenever I need to get back on track, I go for a screen-free walk or allow myself to daydream. We all need to do a lot more daydreaming.

What do you want readers to remember about your books?

That they were able to see themselves or an aspect of themselves in the books, and as a result, they're books they want to share with others.

What would you do if you ever stopped writing?

I hope I never have to find out the real answer to that question, but if I wasn't writing, I'd be teaching in some capacity.

If you were a superhero, what would your superpower be?

Over the years, I've answered this question in many different ways. I've wanted to be able to turn invisible, time travel, shape-shift, and fly (among many others). Right now, I'm thinking I'd want a pause button—the power to stop everything so that I can do all the things I want and need to do, and also to arrange things in the way that I want them to be.

Do you have any strange or funny habits? Did you when you were a kid?

I'll tell you about one I have now: When I lived in the city, I would sometimes go up to the rooftop of my apartment building, plug in my music, and dance like nobody's watching . . . only I know there had to be lots of people watching from other buildings and windows. I'm sure some stranger shot some vid of me doing this and posted it on YouTube. Now I do the dancing-by-myself thing in my backyard.

What do you consider to be your greatest accomplishment?

That's a tough one, but I'll go with a sports one. I ran the New York City Marathon twice. The first time I ran it, I barely even trained. At the time, I wasn't even a runner. I just played basketball and worked out. My friend had an extra number, so I ran with him. When I finished, I was tired, but I actually had a little gas left in the tank. So the next year, I trained and set an ambitious goal. I told myself if met my goal, I'd never run another marathon. I did it!

What would your readers be most surprised to learn about?

Whenever I visit schools, if kids haven't seen a picture of me or visited my website and watched my vids, they're always surprised by my appearance. They don't think I look like a writer . . . whatever a writer is supposed to look like!

Will controversy over standardized testing get in the way of middle-school basketball tryouts, fifth-grade graduation, and a visit from traveling basketball team Hoops Machine?

Keep reading for an excerpt of the next book in the Rip and Red series.

Bubba Chuck

Stumbling over her too-big-for-her-body puppy paws, Bubba chased after the flying Frisbee. When it was almost directly overhead, she sprang off her hind legs, leaped as high as she could, and caught it in her mouth.

"Boo-yah!" I shouted from across the backyard.

"Way to go, Bubba Chuck!" Red shook his fists over his head.

My best friend, Red, calls my new dog by her full name. Red calls everyone by their full name. To Red, I'm Mason Irving. To everyone else, I'm Rip.

"Hand," Red called. He knelt by the steps to the deck and held his open palm next to his knee.

As Bubba galloped back across the yard, her floppy ears and the red Frisbee bounced with each stride.

"Release," Red said firmly when she reached him. "Release."

She dropped the Frisbee into his palm.

"Good girl, Bubba Chuck." He rubbed her head. "Good girl."

I'd been asking Mom and Dad for a dog for a gazillion years. Okay, maybe more like *begging* for a dog for a gazillion years, so when Mom took me to the shelter over Easter vacation, I was mind-blown shocked.

Let me tell you, a five-month-old pit bull mix is the best elementary school graduation present of all time. No doubt!

I leaned back on my hands, kicked out my legs, and crossed my feet. "What are you getting for graduation?" I asked Red.

"I don't know." He shrugged.

"Suzanne better hurry up," I said. Suzanne is Red's mom. "She's running out of time."

"She knows what she's getting me," Red said, "but she won't tell me."

I shook out my dreadlocks. "I'll ask her at dinner tonight."

"She won't tell you."

"Maybe she will." I tossed my Philadelphia 76ers mini basketball from hand to hand. "And when she does tell me, I'm going to torture you with the secret."

We were all going out to dinner tonight—me, Red, Mom, Suzanne, and Dana. Mom and Suzanne have been friends for years. Mom and Dana have been dating since the fall.

"You ready, Bubba Chuck?" Red said, shaking the Frisbee.

He pump-faked once, pump-faked again, and then flung it so it rolled on its edge.

Bubba gave chase, but didn't catch up to the Frisbee until it stopped against the chain-link fence in the back of the yard.

"Come, Bubba Chuck!" Red called.

Bubba shook the Frisbee wildly and then charged back across the yard.

"Release," Red said, holding out his hand.

Bubba gave him the Frisbee.

"Sit." Red raised his palm.

Bubba sat instantly.

"Good, Bubba Chuck," Red said. "Shake." He leaned down and held out his hand.

Bubba slapped her paw into it and toppled over.

Red laughed. "Good girl, Bubba Chuck." He fell onto the grass and hugged her.

Red's amazing with Bubba. I knew he would be, because Red's crazy about dogs. But right now, what was even more amazing was seeing Red rolling around on the grass. It was hard to believe he was the same kid who would bug if you even asked him to sit on the ground a few months back.

"Nice job, Dog Whisperer," I said, crawling over.

Red smiled. "I speak the language of puppies," he said.

"I can't believe we're graduating," I said.

"Two weeks from today, Mason Irving," Red said. "Saturday, June 14, at nine o'clock in the morning is graduation. Saturday, June 14, is two weeks from today."

I rolled onto my back and tossed my Sixers ball into the air. "Gala25 is going to be sick."

"Oh, yeah!" he said. "Gala25 is going to be sick!"

Fifth-grade graduation at Reese Jones Elementary is always a big deal, but this year it's an even bigger deal because it's also RJE's twenty-fifth anniversary. Everyone's coming back for Gala25, the huge anniversary party the night before graduation—former teachers, former students, everyone. Both Suzanne and my mom are on the graduation festivities committee, and lots of parents have been busting their butts the last month putting it all together.

"It's so ridiculous they're making us take another test next week," I said.

"So ridiculous, Mason Irving."

I put down the ball and picked at the grass. "It makes no sense," I said. "Who schedules a test on the Wednesday of the last week of school?"

Like most kids in the galaxy, I can't stand standardized tests. This year, testing week was at the beginning of May, and when I finished taking my last one, I was even more relieved than when the dentist told me at my final checkup that it looked like I would never need braces. But then we found out all the fifth and sixth graders in the state have to take this extra test.

Bubba opened her mouth and reached for my Sixers ball.

"Don't even think it, girl," I said. "That's mine."

"No, Bubba Chuck." Red wagged a finger in front of her snoot. "No."

"You want to know what's going to be the best part of middle school?" I said.

"What's going to be the best part of middle school?"

"I won't have to hang around with you anymore."

Red clenched his fists and tapped his legs. "Very funny."

"Ha! I thought so."

"Well . . . well . . . I won't have to hang around with you anymore, Mason Irving."

You may have noticed by now that Red's quirky. Really quirky. He's on the spectrum. Mom and Suzanne have both tried explaining what that means to me more times than I can remember, but I still don't get it, and to be perfectly honest, I'm not sure the grown-ups who say they know what it means know what it means either.

I do know that not everyone gets Red like I do. And not everyone can joke around with him like I can. You also have to explain a lot of things to Red, but once you do, he gets them and remembers them. Red has a crazy-good memory.

He never forgets things like dates or schedules or the lunch menu at school or basketball stats. *Especially* NBA stats. Red loves the NBA.

Not only is Red my best friend, he's also the best friend you can possibly have.

"Did you see the middle school basketball tryouts announcement?" I said. "They're at the end of summer."

"Only two or three sixth graders make the team, Mason Irving."

"I'm going to be one of them," I said, smacking the ball. "No doubt!"

"No doubt!"

I cupped my hand under Bubba's chin and rubbed my nose against hers. "Red and I are going to be in middle school," I said. "Middle school!"

The Stardust Diner

"Red's present is a surprise," Suzanne said.

"I won't say anything," I said. "I promise."

"Oh, please, Rip," Mom said. "Everyone at this table knows you can't keep a secret from Red."

"Yes, I can." I took a breadstick from the basket and broke it in half. "Don't you understand? I could drive Red crazy with this information."

"Thanks a lot, Mason Irving," Red said.

I bumped his shoulder. "That's what best friends are for."

I'd been trying to convince Suzanne to tell me Red's graduation present from the moment we sat down at our booth at the Stardust Diner. I say *our* booth because the corner booth with the red vinyl cushions next to the old-fashioned jukebox is where we always sit when we come here.

"You'll both find out what it is soon enough," Suzanne said.

"And you won't be
disappointed," Dana added.

"You know too?"

"I do." Dana nodded.

To be perfectly honest, I was pretty sure I knew what
the present was. Make that, I was almost positive I knew,
but I needed confirmation before I could really rub it in
Red's face.

I grabbed a blue crayon from the box the hosters had
given us and began doodling around the edges of my place

mat. Red had started coloring his place mat the second we sat down.

"When was the last time the five of us had dinner together like this?" Suzanne asked.

"I can't remember," Mom said.

"Sunday, April 27," Red said without looking up. "Sunday, April 27, was the last time the five of us had dinner together like this."

"That was the last weekend I had off," Suzanne said. Suzanne's a nurse at a local hospital. "That sounds about right."

"Of course, it's right," I said. "Have you ever known Red to forget a date?"

Ding-dong. Ding-dong.

Mom held up her hands. "That's mine," she said, looking at the phones in the middle of the table. "But I'm not getting it."

"You can," Dana said, smiling.

"It'll cost you if you do," I said. "Ha!"

Ding-dong. Ding-dong.

The use of screens is strictly prohibited during mealtime. That's the rule at both our houses. Mom and Suzanne came up with the rule when Red and I got our cell phones for Christmas. At my house, we keep a metal bucket on the kitchen counter. At restaurants, all screens go in the middle of the table. If someone touches one, that person pays for everyone's meal.

The grown-ups have a harder time with the rule than Red and me. Much harder.

Ding-dong. Ding-dong.

"That phone hasn't stopped all week," Mom said. "In fact, that phone hasn't stopped all month. Everyone needs their graduation questions answered now, now, now."

"Everyone's going to have to wait, wait, wait, Rip's Mom," Red said, still coloring. Red calls my mom Rip's Mom. "If not, you're going to have to pay, pay, pay."

We all laughed.

My mom, Lesley Irving, is a middle school principal a few towns over. Every year at this time, she gets crazy busy because she has to organize her school's graduation, and this year she's doubly busy because she has my graduation, too. Even though there are lots of other parents on the graduation festivities committee, they all bounce everything off Mom because they know she's a principal. Everyone thinks she has all the answers.

When it comes to school stuff, she usually does.

"This RJE graduation is going to be extraordinary," Suzanne said.

"No one will be able to say we're not sending you boys out in style," Mom said. "That's for sure."

I thumped my chest. "That's how it should be."

"I'm working doubles all this week and next," Suzanne said. "That way, I have off the entire weekend."

"I have late nights all this week as well." Mom pointed at Red and me. "That means you two need to go easy on us. No last-minute surprises, you hear that?"

"No last-minute surprises," Red said. "I hear that, Rip's Mom."

"I'm serious, you two," Mom added. "The last weeks of school always worry me."

"Is this where you're going to say something about the school board?" I said.

"Don't get me started," Mom said. "The amount of pushback I've gotten from them trying to coordinate the Gala25 festivities is shameful, and . . ." She wagged a finger at me. "I said, don't get me started. And I mean it, no last-minute surprises. Far too often, someone does something I really wish they hadn't, and then I have to spend way too much time cleaning up the mess.

I reached for another breadstick.

"Honey, that's your last one," Mom said. "You won't have any room for your food."

"I always have room for my food."

"Mason Irving always has room, Rip's Mom," Red said.

I do. I eat everything.

"On second thought," Mom said, smiling, "eat all the breadsticks you want. You're going to need extra energy this week."

"Why's that?"

Mom didn't answer.

"Why's that?" I asked again. "What does that mean?"

She kept smiling her I-know-something-you-don't-know smile and didn't respond.

"Which one of you is reading this?" Dana picked up a book from the cushion beside her.

"I'm reading *Giant Steps* by Kareem Abdul-Jabbar," Red said. He stopped coloring. "Kareem Abdul-Jabbar's a basketball player from back in the day."

"I know who he is," Dana said.

"Kareem Abdul-Jabbar wrote *Giant Steps* while he was still playing basketball for the Los Angeles Lakers." Red spun the crayon on the table. "*Giant Steps* is Kareem Abdul-Jabbar's autobiography."

"He's quite an individual," Dana said. "I bet it's fascinating."

"What are you reading?" Suzanne asked me.

I reached behind me for my book. "*The Boys Who Challenged Hitler.* It's a nonfiction book about World War II."

Nonfiction is my favorite genre. Takara Eid is the one who got me hooked. She's this girl who was in our class back in the fall. Everyone called her Tiki. She loved nonfiction and always posted recommendations on the YO! READ THIS! board in our classroom. It's how I learned about *The Boys Who Challenged Hitler*, and it's how Red learned about *Giant Steps*. But Tiki was only in class for a couple months because her family had to move.

"Do you want to know what the sixth graders told us?" Red asked.

"What sixth graders?" Mom said.

"A bunch of sixth graders came to RJE on Friday to speak to us about middle school," Red answered, still spinning the crayon. "They said if you carry a book wherever you go, you'll never get in trouble."

"Is that so?" Mom said.

"It's so, Rip's Mom," Red said. "They said if you're ever somewhere you're not supposed to be, all you need to do is hold up a book and say you were looking for a quiet place to read."

"Is that so?" Mom said again.

"They said in middle school it's good to be known as the kid who's always carrying a book."

"Call me old-fashioned," Mom said, "but I like to think if you carry a book wherever you go, you'll actually read the book."

"If you carry a book wherever you go, you might read it?" I said, pretending to be surprised. "You will? No way!" I grinned and strummed the table. "Two weeks till graduation!"

"Oh, yeah," Red said. "Two weeks till graduation."

"That means there are still two more weeks of school," Mom said.

I shook out my hair. "There are?"

"There most certainly are," Mom said. "And you still have one more test coming up."

"Thanks for reminding us," I said.

"Yeah, thanks for reminding us, Rip's Mom."

"We shouldn't have to remind you," Suzanne added.

"If you ask me," I said, "I think there should be a

constitutional amendment that says you can't give tests the last week of school."

"No one's asking you," Mom said.

I waved my hand. "School's over."

"No, it is not," Mom said. "You need to take that test seriously."

I strummed the table again. "Two weeks till graduation!"

DON'T MISS THE OTHER ADVENTURES OF RIP AND RED!

"Pure fun with a lot of heart."
—*School Library Journal* on
A Whole New Ballgame